ROCKET CROCKETT

and the

SHANGHAI SHE-DEVIL

PRO SE ⚖ PRESS

ROCKET CROCKETT AND THE SHANGHAI SHE-DEVIL
A Pro Se Press Publication

Edited by Jason Norton and Tommy Hancock
Editor in Chief, Pro Se Productions—Tommy Hancock
Submissions Editor—Barry Reese
Director of Corporate Operations—Morgan McKay
Publisher & Pro Se Productions, LLC-Chief Executive Officer—
Fuller Bumpers

Cover Art by Kristopher Michael Mosby
Print Production and Book Design by Percival Constantine
E-Book Design by Russ Anderson

New Pulp Logo Design by Sean E. Ali
New Pulp Seal Design by Cari Reese

Pro Se Productions, LLC
133 1/2 Broad Street
Batesville, AR, 72501
870-834-4022

editorinchief@prose-press.com
www.prose-press.com

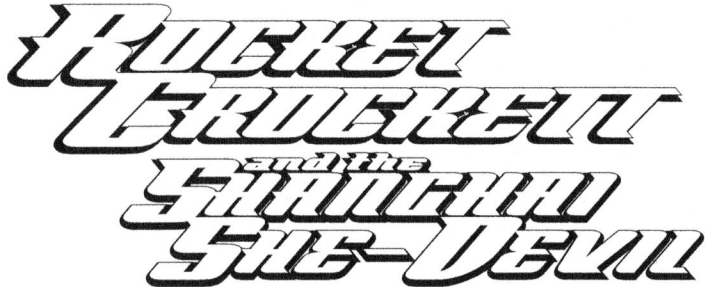

By

Christopher Chambers

PRO SE ⚖ PRESS

Acknowledgements

Many thanks to Tommy Hancock and the folks at Pro Se Productions for introducing me to the pulp universe. Tommy carries the banner for this artform—this literary tradition—whose DNA permeates all species of creative content from books to TV to film to computer gaming. I had never considered the novella/digest novel form before; I'm glad I'm vain enough to have been talked into it!

Thanks also to Jeffrey Schultz, Korean War veteran and retired Chief Petty Officer, U.S. Navy for telling me that historical accuracy can yield to poetry as long as the spirit is true. Kudos to Georgetown University's Lauinger Library for maintaining a universe of knowledge so I can fact-check my imagination. And eternal thanks to my parents, my teachers, friends and family for cultivating that imagination. Storytelling is what makes us human. Embellishing and juicing up the stories is what makes being human exciting…

Finally, I want to thank Ensign Jesse Brown, the U.S. Navy's first black aviator and jet pilot. He died at age 24, in a mission covering the U.S. Marines' withdrawal from the Chosin Reservoir. Through him travels the line that started with the first black seaman fighting beside John Paul Jones in 1779, or defending Washington, D.C., with Commodore Barney in 1814 when our "well regulated militia" was running scared, or manning Union warships in 1864 to free their brethren…to Vice-Admiral Michelle Howard, today. That stunning bravery, perseverance and intelligence on behalf of a nation that shunned or reviled them gave me the inspiration for Rufus Crockett. I just added the spice and swagger...

C.A.C
Washington, D.C.
Summer, 2014

For Spencer

CHAPTER 1

PAPER OVER SHANGHAI

As a burning August melted into a desiccated September, the Korean War scribed a new bloody chapter into the book of death. Gone was the arctic misery, the frozen defeats and frost-bitten retreats of winter past. Gone, too, was Doug MacArthur. Yet without him, the Yanks and their U.N. allies blunted and bludgeoned the marauding horde set loose by Mao and Uncle Joe Stalin to rescue their toady Kim Il-Sung.

The gods of war indeed wrote a new setting for the World War Two-vintage flattop USS *Bonhomme Richard*: the East China Sea.

The East China Sea was a cherry pie-baking spinster, contrasted with her sister, the howling-bitch-in-nylons, smeared-lipstick chippie called the Sea of Japan. The aviators and crew of the "Goodtime Dickie" were happy indeed to be in the tepid, limp grasp of this sister, far from the gales and face-biting sleet hurled by the other.

And there was baseball. Hometown Negro newspapers and newsreels hipped colored dogfaces, swabbies, leathernecks, and airmen to a skinny Giants rookie from Alabama who embarrassed Phillies ace Warren Spahn in Harlem's own Polo Grounds. He wasn't yet as dear as the rival Brooklyn trio of Robinson, Campanella and Newcombe, but his day was coming.

Lt. Rufus Crockett, USN, being a betting man, was

counting on that day coming tomorrow. With a fresh unlit Cuban pinched in his pearly incisors, he called into the mic of his open flight mask, there in cramped bubble top cockpit of his "banjo"—a midnight-gray, straight-winged F2H Banshee called "the Typewriter."

"Control this is Typewriter Four Six Four Tango. The rookie's name is Willie Mays. So if you cats want action on the New York-Pittsburgh game, see 'Bonelip' Broussard in the galley. He's the bank, dig?"

"Get outta here, Four Six Four Tango," griped Combat Control with annoying Bronx spice. "Firstly of all, it don't matter how many spade ballplayers the Giants or the Bums got 'cause allz-youze'll see is Yankee pinstripes come October, *dig*, Mr. *Rocket* Crockett?"

Rocket chuckled until he heard voice he heard in his helmet phones. It was neither Combat Control or the flight boss. It was the flat Ohio drone of Lt. Commander Leiffer, invading the coded frequency.

"Crockett," brayed the Sea Knights squadron leader, "is this gosh-darn chatter what I *think* its about?"

"Say again, Control? Lotta static on this channel..."

"You heard me. *Gambling*...on baseball? And...are you off oxygen? Why aren't you on your mask?"

Because he was below a thousand feet, skimming the gentle swells of the East China Sea. Not a junk or scow in sight.

"Control, this is the Typewriter Four Six Four Tango...gimme my approach vector to target..."

"Typewriter Four Six Four Tango..." moaned Leiffer, as if Rocket was plucking out his finger nails. "...*Crockett*?"

"Going radio silent in t-minus ten seconds—"

Dead air. Rocket's empty wing tanks, which had given him an extra 150 nautical miles from the carrier, fell away.

The jet banked right, rose, then looped into the East China Sea's equally timid baby cousin, the Yellow Sea: so named because of the jaundiced river silt and the dust from faraway exotic deserts which permeated its waters.

"A-ok, daddy-o," whispered Rocket below the cockpit hum and jet stream swoosh, "Special delivery…"

Even at forty miles out, Rocket could see the heat shimmer and coal dust rising from the target: the old colonial trading metropolis of Shanghai.

Chinese coastal radar was primitive, supposedly. Most was captured from Chiang Kai-Shek when he bugged out in '49. Rocket's benefactor, Commander Hank Abensour at the Office of Naval Intel, or ONI, said Uncle Joe Stalin installed some new hardware but never showed Mao how to use it. Some ally Joe turned out to be!

Most of the decent Red pilots, antiaircraft crews and radar were east on the Korean peninsula anyway, not that they did much good. As stalemate settled in along the front, Air Force flyboys in their silver, swept-wing Sabres and those flying castles called B-29s turned the highways and rail lines south from the Yalu River into twisting paths of smoldering metal and charred corpses.

So every junk, ferry, scow, towable sampan, tramp freighter and barge the Chinese could lay their hands on was stuffed with food and ordnance and put out to sea: from Shanghai up to Qingdao, then Qingdao across to Nampho, day and night, to resupply exhausted Commie footsoldiers.

Navy and Marine aviators vowed to sink every damn one of those canoes. Matter of fact, a flight of leathernecks—transferred east from the VMF-311 forward base at Pohang—were off to do the duck hunting maybe a hundred miles north not an hour after Rocket catapulted off the Goodtime Dickie into a sultry headwind.

Rocket's jive was a solo dance. He was to deliver the bad news to the denizens of Shanghai, now likely frying up their pork buns for breakfast, oblivious. Of course bombing China proper was off the table since Harry Truman sent Doug packing.

Yet Rocket wasn't coming in low, fast and *alone* to drop fire on a city swelled to six million souls. There'd been four hitchhikers under the banjo's wings that morning. Two were the fuel tanks now bobbing in the Yellow Sea.

Thousands of leaflets stuffed the other two, still affixed to the Typewriter's pylons.

The "official" side of the sheet blazed with blood-red Chinese characters, translated as: "YOUR SONS AND BROTHERS DIE BY THE THOUSANDS, YET AMERICANS REMAIN! A FREE KOREA REMAINS! THOUSANDS MORE CHINESE WILL DIE, NOT FOR LIBERATION AND REVOLUTION, BUT FOR THE VANITY OF KIM IL-SUNG!"

That's what the US Navy saw: the Chinese side, face-up and loaded for the drop. Delivered by a skiff from Yokosuka Naval Depot, there in Tokyo Bay a week before, and ordered-up by the same CIA boys who'd loved Rocket's jive since he saved the famed Jade Dragon from Reds and *Yakuza*.

Those leaflets about to spill on Shanghai had been "waylaid," however.

The CIA had more important things to worry about than where the truck drivers of their Japanese printing contractors stopped for "refreshment." And, compliments of *Mama-san* Michiko of the Teahouse of the Sublime

Slippery Grip, they did stop, only to have their cargo borrowed by her older brother, Boss Hashimoto, who owed Rocket a favor for liberating much bootleg *sake* from a Shore Patrol raid.

Boss Hashimoto was also smut king of the *Ginza*, and publisher of the most popular skin rag in the Orient, *Nihon Oppai*. Expert four-color lithographer, that *Hashimoto-san*!

The picture and copy he added to the *reverse* side of the propaganda message was an ad for Smoov Mallard Pomade, guaranteed to make even the nappiest hair lay down and shine. With it came a testimonial from Lt. Rufus "Rocket" Crockett, Navy ace jet pilot with that hundred dollar bill smile he only flashed when the bulbs popped…pencil-thin mustache, white silk scarf, G-1 leather flight jacket and combination cap cocked rakishly on a laid down and shiny mane!

The citizens of Shanghai would now know who was strafing their sons and brothers in the trenches, or shooting them out of the sky–and getting paid endorsements for it…

The run took no more than ten minutes, with leaflets falling like tickertape on Broadway. So sharp was Rocket's acumen that not one got wet in the Huanpo or mighty Yangtze River. Rocket even plastered the old colonial buildings along the *Bund*, and made damn sure the Russian Consulate got a few caught in its eaves.

The bulk, however, fluttered into the poorer inland districts as the banjo zoomed along the ramshackle rooftops.

Load spent, Rocket pitched the banjo's nose high to tease smoky blossoms of burst antiaircraft shells and hornet-like tracer fire.

Of the thousands of leaflets settling on the city,

however, there were two—just two—that Rocket would wish hadn't been found.

Usually after these psy-ops runs, Red soldiers in their quilted pajamas and slung *PePeSha* submachine guns would harvest paper, burn it, and shoot anyone caught reading the scraps they'd missed—as if the average peasant or mechanic would be roused or truly able to do anything the leaflet exhorted.

Yet, there was no way Rocket could know that one set of hands grabbing his doctored paper was very small, with fingers and knuckles raw and ashy from the previous day's toils. Those hands quickly stashed the leaflet into a homespun sleeve.

The owner of those hands knew all about the black pilot with the white smile and the laughing eyes. She'd heard he'd done a wonderful thing that far outweighed the death he dealt her countrymen.

News of the warrior Rocket Crockett didn't come by gossip or clandestine radio broadcasts from Hong Kong or Formosa. Rather, it was from her beloved family, who slung kitchen scraps called "chop suey" to Americans, and washed and pressed their shirts there in a far-flung mythic city of crystal and steel called "New York."

And so delicate hands reverently folded the leaflet, and pale lips kissed the sky, for the sky carried love to distant hearts. *I must find him*, the owner of these reverent hands and pale lips prayed to herself. *And when I do, he can rescue Xui-Ling and unite our family…*

The second leaflet found its way to hands anything but delicate, or reverent, or possibly even human. But they were female. *All dame*, as Rocket would say—attached to a lithe and dangerous body softened and scented by oils brewed a thousand years ago.

Those hands crushed the leaflet into a wad, though

not quite a fist could be made around the paper—owing to fearsomely long nails varnished as pearl-white as Rocket's smile on the leaflet, but tipped in crimson paint, as if those very nails had morphed from fashion to feral, and stabbed some helpless prey.

A pigtailed male servant took the wadded page. Rocket, like all Westerners regardless of race or country, figured the pigtail was an anachronism in Mao's worker and peasant paradise.

Not by a longshot. Even the most strident Communists avoided that enclave, nor did the commissars and soldiers disturb the mahjong parlors, fan-tan saloons and brothels over which the mistress of the servant lorded. Just as the scum Japanese left them alone, like the white devil British and the French before them. They knew better.

The servant used the paper as more fuel to feed a fire under a splendid brass tureen, painted with purple orchids. In the tureen, swimming in a sickly piquant broth, a turtle spent its last moments in boiled agony until it belched up its fluid.

Ladling the foul brew into a porcelain cup, the man half-chanted, half-sang the blessing, in Chinese:

"All glory, pearls, ivory, jade and coin to the Orchid Tong

Long life to Mother Blossom

The Dowager Wife of Our Master and Father Blossom

For She shall reign as Queen of White Powder."

The cup of evil nectar passed to dagger-nailed hands, and the cup, in turn, rested on lips painted black. The woman gulped. Once sated, she tossed the cup onto the floor, angrily.

"I must find him," the owner of these deadly hands and stygian lips hissed…in perfect English. "And when

I do, I myself will bind Rocket Crockett, and administer the thousand cuts until he has no flesh on his bones..."

CHAPTER 2

YELLOW SEA JUMP N'

JIVE

At 14,000 feet, Rocket stashed his cigar in his leather flight jacket and clipped on his oxygen mask. The second he broke radio silence with the flattop, his helmet sputtered and popped with cries and shouts.

It was the Marines, the boys from VMF-311. Six of them, in F9F Panthers, gung-ho to tear up that big juicy Qingdao-Nampho convoy. The Panther was one of the Navy's old straight wing jets, like Rocket's banjo. A little more pugnacious, not as graceful.

And there was jumpin' n' jivin', all right. Rocket winced as he heard the aviators call out the bandits. Six...no, eight...wait, ten...twelve...*more?*

It was an ambush, with the convoy as bait.

Pouncing from their cover in the cloud tops were deadly MiG-15 jets and at least six or seven Yak-9s. The Yaks were Russian World War Two piston-driven prop fighters, but they were heavily armed and fast enough to corral the Panthers into an aerial killing box for the nasty little MiGs to finish off.

"*Bonhomme Richard...*" snarled Rocket, ready to chew his own guts to help his fellow aviators, "...this is Typewriter Four-Six-Four-Tango on channel five-three. Gimme an inbound vector on this fight. Am climbing to my ceiling and pushing the throttle hard on account of these Marines being in deep, deep *kimchi*!"

9

"Roger, Typewriter, this is Combat Control," answered the carrier, the Bronx vinegar drained from his voice, as the flattop was impotent to help the imperiled Marines. "On my mark; we gotcha at forty nautical miles south by southwest of their last signal, thirty-six miles northeast of Daecheong Island weathership beacon. Their Combat Air Control is Marine Air Station Osan, channel six-zero, copy?"

Unfortunately, the next voice Rocket heard belonged to his C.O.

"You menace!" spat Leiffer over the frequency. "I don't care how the brass wants to show you off in *Stars and Stripes* or colored crowds back home! You're bound for the brig for this stunt, Mister! The hangar crew found a spare bundle of your counterfeit leaflets with your shoe-shine boy grin on them!"

Men were dying and this ofay is wolfing over Smoov Mallard pomade? Rocket growled inwardly.

"Am homing in on their signal as best I can," pleaded Rocket, ignoring Leiffer's bile, "but they are going to be slaughtered if I don't have tactical guidance on the situation…"

Suddenly, Rocket heard static and a different voice, breaking in from the Goodtime Dickie's navigation bridge.

"Rocket, this is Captain Connor," barked the old man. "Son, it's gonna take every chit in Asia I got to keep you from being clapped in irons once you drop your tailhook…but for now… stand by for vector and coordinates from Osan. Blast those sumbitches outta' the sky!"

"Aye-Aye, *Bonhomme Richard*. Am hot and ready."

Rocket heard a heavy sigh from Captain Connor. "One more thing, son. No help from us, but the Air Force boys are on an intercept…twenny-one minutes…"

"Understood."

Twenty-one minutes. Everyone would be dead in ten. And Rocket's banjo was low on 20mm and .50 caliber ammo—removed to lighten the jet for its long-range psy-ops run.

No matter. Rocket gained as much altitude as he dared, leveled, then vectored-in on the battle. Thirty miles out…fifteen…then, below and at his 9 o'clock, he saw giant curly-cue vapor trails, puffs of smoke, and flashes of tracer and 20mm cannon rounds.

Two Panthers, already shot up, tried to decoy to the Reds from their beleaguered comrades. Another Panther had bought it and went down into the Yellow Sea, its aviator already dead at the stick before impact.

One wounded Panther called, "This is Zulu Bravo Seven Five." Rocket could the taste the bitter cocktail of fear and despair in the Marine's voice. "My wingman's down…am leaking fuel…guns are jammed…may have to ditch…"

Three of the Yaks and two MiGs had bought it, too. But that left maybe a dozen bandits closing in to kill the last two Panthers.

"Zulu Bravo Seven Five…this is the Typewriter. You leathernecks always need the Navy to pull your draws outta the shit, eh?"

"Ha!" exclaimed the Marine, as terror evaporated for an instant. "I could kiss ya!"

Yeah and you'd be arrested in good ole Tennessee for that.

Rocket turned the banjo into a figure eight, mimicking the MiG "hold- to-attack" pattern taught by Russian honchos. "Okay fellas, this is the Typewriter," he called. "Comin' out of the sun. *Tap, tap, tap,* baby…"

In a screaming dive, the banjo burst from the sun's blinding glare and latched onto a MiG's 6 o'clock. The silvery little gremlin exploded with one burst from Rocket's cannon.

Rocket pulled heavy G's in a left bank, then gained altitude for speed and another attack...but not before flaming a Yak-9 crossing his path. The pilot popped his canopy and jumped—his chute opening as the fighter's tail broke apart.

"I'll bust up that cat again next time I see him," chortled Rocket as he once more used the sun and high haze as cover.

Down again he dove, guns blazing, until the cannon was drained and all that was left were his twin .50s.

Scratch another MiG.

But before Rocket could pull up, a new MiG stapled itself to the Typewriter's tail.

Oh, we gonna dance...

Rocket broke left to dodge a line of tracer and a pop of 20mm fire. A lucky cannon round chewed into the banjo's dark gray fuselage. It didn't puncture the armor under Rocket's rear end, but landed close enough to dry what had been a wet mouth, and almost moisten what had been a dry seat!

The banjo plummeted, nose to the waves to shake the MiG, but the Commie pilot stayed glued to Rocket while a comrade darted up from the battle's floor, hoping to hit Rocket dead ahead or at least force him out of the dive so he'd be easy pickings for his friend.

Right ploy, wrong time. A Panther daisy-chained on the pursuing MiG, fired, and drew smoke.

With the chasing MiG hastily breaking off, Rocket tightened both his jaw and his fundament, for he'd only have a few seconds to fire the shorter-range machine guns then pull up before he hit either the on-rushing MiG or the water.

He jammed on the trigger. The MiG's single-nostril intake broke up in a flash of fire.

Rocket sprung his speed brakes, flaps, and yanked the stick –anything to bleed his frightful momentum. The Gs almost ghosted his head but somehow, he recovered in time to look back at the spray kicked up from his jet wash on the waves.

The Air Force's Sabres arrived like John Wayne and Henry Fonda on cavalry steeds, scattering the surviving MiGs and Yak-9s. After driving off the enemy, the little Sabres did what they could on the convoy, shooting up a two-stack freighter, sinking a tanker and two junks.

Jockeying one of the Sabres was good ol' Chappie, glad that another dusky derring-doer of the sky was up there with him.

"You got a mean machine there, young brother Crockett," cheered the Air Force's most deadly colored ace in Rocket's helmet.

"Ain't the machine that's deadly, baby," corrected Rocket. " It's the cat holdin' the stick an' thumbin' the trigger."

Gum-beating was short-lived, for the Typewriter was flying on fumes. With the carrier too far away, the Sabres escorted the banjo, along with the remaining Panthers, to the small Marine airfield near Osan. Chappie did a wing dip as Rocket dropped his gear, then the Air Force boys shot off into the wild blue yonder.

On the ground, dozens of bare-chested, unshaven grunts joined the ground crews cheering and shouting even as the Typewriter's jet wash kicked up the summer dust.

Popping his canopy after taxiing to the parking

circle, Rocket watched the throng of men in dirty olive drab surge to his plane—though wisely avoiding the still-spinning fans inside the front wing scoops. He gave a thumbs-up, unbuckled himself and rose in his seat.

The din quieted for an instant when Rocket unclipped his mask and yanked off his flight helmet.

He heard, "Hang me if he ain't a nigger…?"

Nervously, one of the ground crewmen slid a steel ladder to the cockpit and Rocket climbed down to the murmuring, nonplussed Marines.

"Who the hell is that guy?" one voice whined above the utterances.

"He's the spade Navy flyer…" another joined, "… what's his name?"

Then another voice huffed, "Crockett 'Rocket' Crockett? Holy shit, *that's* the colored guy they been jawboning about?"

Finally, a skinny Marine with a coal black complexion and a broad smile under the sweat-stained visor of his field cap elbowed in.

"*Damn right* that's him!" gushed the colored grunt. He saluted Rocket, as did the few other Negroes present and a handful of white Marines.

Rocket returned the salute, yet remained cool as a fan for the stunned and angry men who still couldn't believe their eyes. Damned if he was going to face a lynch party after the morning he'd had!

Suddenly three Marine aviators pushed through the crowd, still toting their helmets. Though exuberant, they jumped to attention as soon as Rocket's icy countenance met theirs.

Yet Rocket recognized one of them instantly, and forgot his "rule about cool;" don't smile unless someone's taking your picture.

"Major Ted Williams," crooned the Marine with a perfect sun tan and perfect haircut. The Red Sox slugger saluted, then grabbed Rocket's hand. "And I am extremely grateful."

Rocket was rarely star-struck. There was that time at the Harlem Canteen when Lena Horne dropped in to meet servicemen shipping out to Korea. This was one of those rare times.

"Officer on deck, Marines!" Williams hollered to those men still idle or murmuring.

Quickly, even the hold-outs in that surly crowd saluted. Some just accepted it, some were still begrudging and quietly cursing.

Rocket pulled out the Cuban he'd mouthed up in the heavens. The other aviator, the callow fellow who said he'd kiss his rescuer, drew his Zippo and lit Rocket's stogie. After savoring a puff, Rocket returned the salute to the rest of the gathered company. *Yeah, they got the message, all right.*

The third Panther jockey was bashful, yet all smiles. Rocket offered him a draw on the Cuban, but the man shook his head.

His refusal wasn't for the reason Rocket and the colored Marines there may have thought.

"Sorry Lieutenant," declined the leatherneck aviator. "I don't smoke. Just wanted to thank you in the flesh, though. Name's John Glenn."

"You're the one who daisy-chained the MiG on my ass, right?"

Glenn nodded, humble with his own skill and certainly embarrassed by Rocket's colorful language. With an abundance of grace for a Marine, he introduced Rocket to the base C.O.

"Lieutenant!" trumpeted the barrel-chested honcho

after shaking Rocket's hand, "we're hoping you'll join us for lunch in the officers' hooch across from hangar." A Marine in an apron answered a query by saying lunch was spam and succotash. "Ah crap. Well, we got cold beer, at least."

Clucking his tongue Rocket nodded.

"Cold beer'd be great, Major, but after that I need to get patched up, refuel and get back to my carrier. I would, though, like to impose on Mr. Williams and ask for his autograph, though I don't much like the American League, ya know what I'm sayin'?"

The "Splendid Splinter" gave Rocket a wink, understanding full-well Rocket's dig. "We'll get our colored ballplayers soon enough, Lieutant," he said as he pulled a ball point pen from his green flight suit.

That'd be worth some money in Tokyo, Rocket mused.

The lanky black Marine who'd first spoken approached as Williams handed Rocket the prize.

"Sir, *we'd* be mighty honored if you'd stop by, have some chow with us." Then the man leaned close, whispering, "You know how these Koreans love swine more than us folk, so we got some trotters barbequing."

This awakened the Memphis boy in Rocket.

"Y'all got real hot sauce for them pig knuckles?"

"Yessir, straight from Loo-siana."

"Ain't gotta invite me twice, cuz."

Before going wheels up and banking south over the sea, Rocket hoisted cold Carlings with the white flyers and station officers. Many of these men had trained at Cherry Point, North Carolina, where the only Negroes on base were civilians collecting garbage and painting fences, so having Rocket around seemed like having Joe Louis visit.

The Black Buccaneer of the Atmosphere kept

his appetite for some pig knuckles with the colored leathernecks, and as payment doled out shiny new tins of Smoov Mallard he always carried in his flight suit.

Most of the Marines declined Rocket's offer, as Smoove Mallard was already a staple of care packages from home. Still, a few ran to their kits and fetched their own faded tins and asked Rocket to put his John Hancock on them, just as he had asked the Red Sox star.

"Where're your peoples from, Lt. Crockett?" nudged a private seated on a bench next to Rocket as he autographed the dingy, dinged cans. The man had been rubbing liniment on his cracked toes and heels while his some of his comrades shagged fly balls or lolled in the shade with their hot sauce and trotters.

"Tennessee, but I'm sure not related to Davey Crockett." After a chuckle with the men he added, "Went to college at Howard University, Washington, D.C. Stuck around Washington longer than I should have, however."

"Family there?" chimed in another black Marine.

Rocket smiled, shook his head. His head kept the memory of Brenda, who yes was still there in the Nation's Capital, in the tidy rowhouse purchased by the good Dr. Frank Goins. Beautiful views of the campus and earshot of baseball and the gridiron at Griffith Stadium. Two little sons, neither with Rocket's face, though she told him once, in a moment of shame, she wished they had.

"How 'bout back in Memphis, sir?"

"My mom and daddy, Viola Jean and Reverend Samson Crockett, Sr." He paused, "…and my brother Sammy. He's dead."

The colored leathernecks ran through the usual causes: chain gang or police, rail accident or farm mishap?

Rocket lied a little, truthed a little.

"He was a pilot…in the Navy we say 'aviator.' 332nd Fight Group, P-41 then P-51 Mustang jockey. Trained down Tuskegee…killed a lotta Krauts. Was ready to come out here to kill a lotta Japs but the A-bomb ended that. He, um… died in a plane crash training new pilots."

It was not the time to talk truth. No one wanted to hear about a knotted rope slung over a buzzing old gaslight pole, and body hanging there, stripped of its uniform and medals.

Bravado was always refuge, however. With a grin Rocket said to the dark-skinned, lanky Marine turned out to be a sergeant, "You the only cat here who ain't asked me for a autograph, yet you invited me over here, hooked me up with some hot sauce and pig knuckles…"

The Marine who'd smiled all afternoon sudden grew grim, sullen. Scratching his stubble-sprouted chin, he explained, "They're trucking all of us back into action next week. They say they say we gonna hit the 'Punchbowl.' I figger signatures ain't gonna be much use on them hills and ridges unless it can requisition us a couple more flamethrowers, Lieutenant. We goin' toe-to-toe with them Chinese: bayonets and brass knuckles."

When he'd found Sammy's body…when Brenda'd told him to get lost because she needed a man she could count on—these were the only times Rocket felting insignificant, weak. Until now.

Rocket pasted on a smile, said good-bye and hailed a jeep back the airfield.

"There is one thing, though, sir," called the thin sergeant, stopping Rocket before he could climb into the jeep. "If you can swing it—somebody like you can get these boys some *baseball* autographs, right?"

"Um…I guess…sure. Who ya want?"

"That boy Willie Mays. But it looks like Jackie's

gonna take the pennant from them."

That's when Rocket knew most of these men would never leave the Punchbowl, just as the East China Sea would hoard the skeletons of men and machines beneath her sweet and tranquil waves.

Suddenly, this war was no longer Rocket's personal jump n' jive.

CHAPTER 3

IN THE LAIR OF THE SHE-DEVIL

Meanwhile, as Rocket banked the banjo over Osan then out to sea to rendezvous with the carrier, there were deeds both selfless and foul in the slums of Shanghai which would hook Rocket like an invisible claw.

With the paper proclaiming Rocket's face still tucked in a wide sleeve, a teenage girl named Mewo darted and dodged through the evening market crowd, jamming the *shikumen* alley above which she lived.

Usually the only signs of life at dusk were dogs lapping greedily from fetid puddles or running for their lives from the stew pot, or People's Liberation Army goons sporting blue armbands, making sure peasant and laborer alike remained indoors after a random and shifting curfew time.

But that evening, makeshift tables cobbled from old doors and scrap timber featured melons, duck eggs –but no ducks–, mushrooms, pears, a few sacks of rice flour and beans here and there, and some sticks hung with still squirming pomfret and eels. It was a cornucopia after a year of want despite the propaganda blaring victory and revolution, and everyone was outdoors.

If only the leaflet had *just* the man's face and not the defeatist message on the reverse side, Mewo would have been be a lot less nervous. It seemed that every soldier she passed looked her up and down. Perhaps it was her hare's pace and quick cuts; perhaps it was that she was very pretty—almost a twin to her older cousin Xui-Ling.

Yes, she was small, but, like Xui-Ling, men always tried to imagine the form under her loose homespun, and, just like Xui-Ling, she eschewed pigtailed braids like the other girls at the factory wore for thick bangs and a self-cut bob. Girls even gave her Xui-Ling's nickname, because of that hair style: Shih Tzu.

Mao and General Secretary Zhou had labeled as traitors all who fled with Chiang and his Kuomintang to Formosa. Never mind that Xui-Ling and her father, Ri Huang, left through Portuguese Macau and never set foot on counter-revolutionary "Taiwan," or that Uncle Ri, side-by-side with the Communists, bled to free China from the Japanese.

No, Uncle Ri worked as a *sous-chef* on a floating Macau restaurant, serving fat *tai pan* foreigners and Western spies. That alone made him guilty of treason.

Gossip sprouted in those blighted alleys—planted and fertilized by the Changning District's commissars – held that Ri's daughter, Xui-Ling Huang, was now "Julie Wang," and her home was Ri's capacious flat with its own bathroom and electricity. She wore high heels and make-up and watched Hollywood movies in air-conditioned theaters and drove motorcars over vast bridges to islands of skyscrapers and made love to rich white men and musical Negroes—whoever met her fancy at the moment.

Warring amongst themselves, then with the Japanese, then with each other again and now with the United Nations, had scattered millions of Chinese to the four winds. The only means of communication was what the old folks cleverly called the "bamboo telegraph" of family networks. This web had nothing to do with espionage or war, Nationalists or Communists. This was an underground railroad of messages keeping far-flung families linked to Chinatowns all over the globe. Through it, Mewo was able to get word out that she and her younger siblings were now orphans.

But in China, there was *yin* to every *yang*. The bamboo telegraph also carried the grabbing, sucking tentacles of a vast, voracious kraken of crime. And Mewo knew the truth. There weren't Hollywood movies for her cousin "Julie," for she and her father suffered the rasping clutches of one such tentacle.

The junk to Fuzhou was going to putter away at sunset—and the sun was dimming fast in the west. As the first street lights sputtered to life, Mewo sprinted below the suspicious eyes of soldiers acting as traffic cops.

She arrived at the Huangpu River quay, soaked with sweat and breathless just as the shadows settled over the old European buildings of the *Bund*.

The Huangpu, a tributary of the irrepressible Yangtze, was where north and south China met, literally. From the north came millet, soybean oil and coal. Much of the burden for the rest of the trip south was on junks sailing to Fuzhou then down the coast. The ships visited islands close to Hong Kong and Kowloon, and often docked to trade in Macau for hard currency. Such was the first leg of the bamboo telegraph.

The trade coming up from the south, however, was all rice. Tons of it.

Yet mixed in with the loads of China's ancient staple were two other products: one old, familiar, the other a mysterious infant which one day would be more valuable than opium.

The familiar product was gold, cash—even American

dollars—stuffed in rice sacks and loaded on rolling stock to Beijing; stuck in cargo hold and sailed east to Chiang's Taiwanese government in rebel Taipei. Working both sides shocked no one in Shanghai.

And everyone benefitted from that other, newer product growing brazenly in the humid valleys of the Yunnan Province, all the way to the jungles of French Indochina, Burma and Thailand: poppies. Or rather, the juice from the fecund wombs of those mother blossoms, distilled in morphine, then milled in the white powder temples of Shanghai...

Standing at the quay's edge was the man called Dockmaster Xi. His pudgy, pitted face, under bite and bald pate, lit by the pallor of greenish lights, made him look like a giant toad wearing dusty human trousers and a black *changshan* . He spit phelgmy brown streams of *binlang* chew onto the crumbling concrete to punctuate the shouts at his hulking underlings who collected kickbacks and guarded the contraband.

Dockmaster Xi was also the gatekeeper of messages in the bamboo telegraph. The typical payment to send personal notes, photos and documents was ten yuan plus a favor. If valuables like jewelry were to be smuggled in a can of soybean oil, it was twenty yuan and a favor.

For this toad, the favor was more than a kiss behind the columns of the warehouses of the quay, and it made Mewo vomit afterward. Xui-Ling had probably experienced far worse, so Mewo would always close her eyes and think of her.

"Most beneficent Dockmaster," tempted Mewo, trying to be coquettish despite her encroaching nausea. "I have a flowerto deliver to a most sublime florist where the Jesus cross reflects over the water."

That was code for the ruins of St. Paul's Cathedral

in Macau.

"What is it this time, my little Shih Tzu, huh?" snorted the gangster after spitting another disgusting brown spot onto the ground. "Lemme see?"

Mewo hesitated, then produced the leaflet with the propaganda side up.

"Are you daft, girl? You want to bring the heat down on us?"

She flipped it and pointed to the black American's smiling face. The toad's eyes widened.

"Wait…um…who's it going to?"

She giggled, nudging him playfully to throw him off.

"You never asked for that before. My relatives will know who must get it, but it is probably safer to for them to receive it, once in America, at *this* place…"

With her finger, Mewo traced the address of the Smoov Mallard headquarters on the bottom of the advertisement. Broadway and 143rd Street, New York, New York. Telephone Hamilton 7-0999. She knew it to be the place where her family lived, called "Harlem."

Dockmaster Xi couldn't read English to save his dreadful soul, but he'd sure as sin seen Rocket's face before. Not like the thousands of Shanghai residents had seen it that morning—before hurriedly tossing the papers in rubbish piles as soldiers approached.

No, the Dockmaster saw that face when another leaflet just like Mewo's was held in front of his own face and the faces of dozens of hoodlum captains not hours before!

This would win him great face.

"Gimme the piece of paper… and your money," croaked the toad.

"N-No…*favor*?" The thought of his hands on her body sickened Mewo, and she had to smile again to mask her nausea.

"Beat it before I change my mind."

Barely containing her relief, Mewo supplicated, backed away, then ran home.

"Pack this with oil cans," directed the Dockmaster to a henchman as Mewo disappeared.

"But maybe we take it to White Paper Fan first?"

"Do it! We can always find out who the little cur is trying to reach. We are the Orchid Tong! We can find anyone, anywhere!"

The Dockmaster didn't bother containing his glee as he summoned a barefoot man tugging a rickshaw—another anachronism Mao supposedly had expunged—climbed in, almost breaking the axle and the man's back, then screamed for the human taxi to take him through the the Bund and back into the slums.

Yet his destination was a palace in the blight. It sprawled across three blocks, and was covered with a magnificent gabled roof as if a pagoda of old. Dragon and phoenix figures were carved into the stone corbels where the roof timbers met brick and stone.

A lone guard sporting criss-crossed ammo bandoliers stood behind a spotlight illuminating an iron gate to a courtyard. He had an ancient curved and serrated sword in one hand…and fingered a 9mm machine-pistol in the other. He jerked a nod and the Dockmaster entered.

The only light in the room the toad entered was from the dozens of incense sticks and oil lamps dotting bamboo planks leading to a set of steps, similarly lined with lamps and brass incense holders.

The panels of the room were open to the muggy night breeze, sending the jasmine and myrrh scent wafting high, though not enough to blow out the flames. Curtain panels of purple and green flapped. Such was the only noise until...

"Dockmaster Xi," chirped a shrill male voice from the darkness. "So you are certain this waif wanted to contact the Negro?"

"Y-Yes. All glory and coin to the Mother B-Blossom and..."

"Calm yourself."

The disembodied voice materialized as a short, slight man in a tan double-breasted business suit and spectator shoes, an orchid pinned to his lapel. Tortoiseshell spectacles rested on a pug nose and covered narrow eyes. slicked black hair, so slick it could've made Rocket give up Smoov Mallard!

The man smiled. Each tooth was silver and caught the glint of candlelight.

The toad never met White Paper Fan, chief accountant, face-to-face, but he'd heard the stories about how the man had his teeth broken out twice. First, by the Japanese in 1938... and again by Kuomintang soldiers during the civil war, who pulled out each of his ivory crowns one by one, thus gaining him much face with the Communists.

He opted for silver now.

"Did I do well?" fished the toad. "I mean...I didn't bring the paper because it had some writing on it..."

"Hmmm, the propaganda..."

"N-No...something else," stammered Dockmaster Xi, "scribbled...by the little bitch. Part of a message, I guess. But...I will know to where it will be delivered... I can have men follow it."

White Paper Fan approached, shaking his head. "Is that your job—tracking shipments and messages overseas. Doing...*intelligence* work?"

"Uh..no, I'm not intelligent. But—"

"Precisely," mocked White Paper Fan. "And this girl who made the drop. All you have is a nickname—*Shih Tzu*? And no ultimate destination for this message?"

"Apologies."

"You have one job," snapped White Paper Fan. "A job *many* would like to have in these hard times. Yet still…" White Paper Fan's tone switched from sinister anger to jocular camaraderie. He patted the toad on his lumpy shoulders, then folded his arms and paced away as if he were a proud boss. "…you exhibited initiative, and you remembered our rather hasty and vague directive from this morning after the American's flight. How shall we reward you?"

Showing his *binlang*-stained teeth, the Dockmaster said, "Maybe...maybe travel to Hong Kong to see the girls, gamble? Maybe even… *America*…like you do sometimes?"

Though nodding along to the gibberish, White Paper Fan's eyes shifted to the steps leading up to the curtained platform within the great hall. Another figure had been waiting and listening. In the dark.

"Then so be it," whispered a feminine voice, silken and venomous.

The toad turned, searched the stairs and saw her. He dropped to one knee, trembling.

Down the steps, slowly, she floated. As she came into the meager light, Dockmaster Xi saw that her face was painted white as a ghost's, lips stained black. Her body was draped in a shimmery green *chang-ao* embroidered with purple orchids and black dragons. A long dagger pinned a phoenix crown dripping with pearls and onyx beads to her tower of black hair.

She halted above her quaking underling. "Rise, Dockmaster Xi, so I may bless you."

The toad got off his haunches but would not raise his gaze to his mistress. She withdrew a hand from the folds of her gown and slowly unsheathed her nails. They clacked as she extended her palm. With a pointed index finger, she placed the tip of her claw under his chin to coax it up.

She drew very close, as if to kiss him. His ugliness and foul breath did not repulse her.

"Perhaps you could have switched the document and brought the original here, or even had the foresight, many times before, to ascertain the real name of the waif who delivered it…rather than forcing your beastly self on her young body."

"As…as I reported to White Paper Fan, I-I didn't touch her this time…"

Her lips almost touched his pitted cheek.

"*Shush*. Rest easy, we will find her. We will find the Negro. We will find the recipient. Because of you. And, ironically, in spite of you. Given that *yin* and *yang*, your reward will be smaller."

Pulling her nail away, she coaxed a tiny drop of blood under the Dockmaster's chin.

The toad smiled despite the twinge of pain, then said, "Thank you, Dowager…"

He looked puzzled, for a moment, when the floor opened up beneath his feet. His eyes widened and he screamed as he fell, until one of the many iron spikes that tore into him on impact drove into the occipital curve of his skull, silencing him in this life, but not in the many hells to come.

"Take his manhood," commanded the bloodthirsty Dowager, Mother Blossom of the Orchid Tong. "Pickle it, then show it to this waif who he defiled once you find her so she may have peace before she's killed. I'm going to bathe, wash my hair. It's been a trying day."

White Paper Fan nodded as he dabbed some perspiration with his pocket square. He shouted for the Dowager's pigtailed retainers to peel yet another errant employee from the skewers in the cellar.

*****

When the night grew darker but not cooler, the Dowager returned without her ancient costume and crown.

Rather, she'd sheathed herself in something more modern: a scarlet, body-clinging *cheongsam* stitched with gold orchids. The thigh-high slit that climbed up the side of the dress teased at a well-placed stocking garter. Farther up, her bosoms strained the fabric like two oriental artillery shells.

She'd flung off the dainty lotus slippers for a pair of crimson stiletto heels. A single purple orchid anchored her upswept hair. Yet her lips remained black.

Permanently black.

She motioned to White Paper Fan as a servant placed a cigarette in a polished mahogany holder and lit it.

"You are my brains, White Paper Fan," purred the Dowager. She exhaled a smoke ring, then twiddled the cigarette holder in her long nails. "Now educate me."

The dapper flunky bowed as his mistress alighted like a lithe tigress on a tufted chaise, her long legs slightly crossed so the slit in her *cheongsam* would reveal enough…but not all.

"Mother Blossom, we will cast a wide net for any girl nicknamed Shih Tzu. Wide casting takes time…and the other tongs will be suspicious."

"Bah…to the Hell of Peeled Eyeballs with the other

tongs," huffed the Dowager, now making love to her sexy form and exotic face in a mirror next to the chaise. "I do not want the messenger necessarily. I want the recipient…and the subject."

"What we have now is the middle," answered White Paper Fan with a cloying tone and smile. "From the Dockmaster's mumblings it appears this girl sends messages to America through Macau. We have nothing beyond that. Once we extract the middle's significance, the beginning and end will be but mere a pleasant opening and closure—as a scallion cake starts a fine meal and the sugar dumpling concludes it."

"Pretty words," snarled the Dowager. "I've skinned men alive for offering pretty words without facts or results."

"Understood, Mother Blossom," her executive cringed. "But…consider this humbly offered alternative: there may not be any connection with this man Crockett other than novelty, gossip."

The Dowager lifted herself to the ridge of the chaise, her back arched, black lips curled, and flawless white teeth bared.

"*Or…*" White Paper Fan wisely retreated, "someone is trying to get him a message and this is the only channel available to the poor ignorant sots..."

The Dowager smiled, springing off the chaise. She came close to White Paper Fan, straightening his tie and pocket square as he swallowed nervously.

"See?" whispered the She-Devil, throatily yet playfully. "It pays to be paranoid. That is why my kind has outlived the Mongols, the Manchus, the British pigs who educated you, the French, the silly Boxers, that dreamer Sun, the damn Japs, and that vain idiot Chiang and his tiresome social climbing wife. Now the Reds seek my favor…and I shall outlive them, too."

She released White Paper Fan from her hold, then sashayed around the room, continuing her sermon.

"The poppy is our newly-birthed mother blossom. Rufus Crockett almost aborted her. His interference has allowed the Italians to remain on their throne in New York."

It was as if a flashbulb went off in White Paper Fan's head.

"If I may, my Dowager…what about New York? Many of these family messages end up there."

"Oh to the Hell of Burrowing Imps with New York," discounted Mother Blossom, twirling to locate a cocktail. "Chinese are keen for New York because San Francisco is too much like home. You forget, I have seen Canal Street in New York with my late husband… when it was, indeed, a canal…so long ago. It remains a sty, I hear… with Italian pigs in their shiny shoes rooting on the other side of it."

"Not *Canal Street*, mistress. To where are Crockett and his tribesmen drawn, as are ants to rotten fruit? And to where is our new mother blossom to sprinkle her bounty?"

"*Harlem…*"

"Yes, mistress," nodded White Paper Fan with a silvery grin. "I think you have narrowed our search." He turned to screech at suited underlings waiting outside the room. "Send a wire to Kowloon, for relay to America, to the dog who calls himself 'Larry Ma,' at the Wing Fat Sino-American Trading Company, New York. Then activate our spy. There is but one route the Negro devil has if leaves Korea and returns home…"

The She-Devil pursed her black lips, as if making love to an unseen demon, then smiled.

Chapter 4

The Ballroom Blaze

A s the late summer sun set fire to the East China
Sea, green-smocked flight deck crewman folded
the Typewriter's wings like a giant roosting bat's. The
jet rode the massive elevator from the flight deck to the
Goodtime Dickie's cavernous hanger deck.

Rocket saluted his steed for bringing him back alive,
then reported to the fantail for the bad news. Captain
Connor had convened a board of inquiry, meeting on the
flag bridge in the carrier's tower, 1530 hours the next
day. Rocket was confined to quarters until then.

And so, when the day of reckoning came. Rocket
arrived on the flag bridge in his summer service dress
khaki uniform and black necktie. He sat stiff before the
men who were both feting him for valor…and cajoling
him for plastering Communist China with thousands of
advertisements featuring his face. The two bars on his
shoulder boards were no match for the scrambled eggs,
gold and silver leaves, eagles and one star of his judges.

The star belonged to Rear Admiral Burke, who
thought the incident with the leaflets serious enough
to ferry over from the cruiser *St. Paul* to visit. That a
colored aviator was involved made it imperative to nip
this issue in the bud fast.

Still, the inquiry was just that: a panel, not a courts-
martial, as Lt. Commander Leiffer had threatened when

he discovered the stray stack of adulterated leaflets. There was no reading of charges or a stenographer. Indeed, there was only Commander Hollins, Goodtime Dickie's X.O., taking notes and also acting as panel member.

Admiral Burke sat at the center of a long table, flanked by Captain Connor on his left;

to his right sat Commander Harry Abensour, Office of Naval Intelligence.

Abensour was Rocket's under-the-table C.O.—when Rocket was loaned out to the spy boys. And was the only Naval officer Rocket knew who came to the war *already* with a mustache…other than himself. Once, to establish a rapport with his young black asset, Abensour joked that facial hair was something swarthy Spanish Jews and Negroes alike did to flout their outsider status. He was cagey and not by the book. So why was he there as an inquisitor?

Captain Connor settled back in his chair and groaned in his gravelly Texas voice, "Rocket, what are we gonna do with you? Hell, you're our own jet-propelled Jackie Robinson, and there're more of you boys coming. But son, poking at the ugly underbelly of this Navy and this war while whistling by as both isn't the same thing as winning." He then looked to Admiral Burke, "Arleigh, I believe you had some issues to cover."

Admiral Burke nodded and said, "First, I have here a telegram from the Boston Red Sox organization. I quote the material part: '…a most sincere thanks from the People of Boston to Lt. Rufus Crockett, USN, CVA USS *Bonhomme Richard*, for his bravery in rescuing Major Ted Williams,' etc. etc. '…Lt. Crockett is a credit to his race and the United States Armed Forces.' Sadly there is a also non-sequitur at the end—something about how this message shall be not be construed as support for the

Boston Red Sox obtaining Negro ballplayers."

"Begging the admiral's pardon," offered Rocket, "but why tell me that?"

"Because I empathize, Mr. Crockett. The intolerable pressure of being an aviator, being colored…it must create steam to blow off, thus tempting you with…well…frolics and detours."

"Sir…are you asking me to admit I need a psyche leave?"

"Mister," sighed the admiral, "if that works to quell the rumblings out there, than that is what you will do if you know what's good for you." Then Burke's face hardened. "Under ordinary circumstances, I'd bust you to mess boy. But nothing about you is remotely ordinary."

Amen, Rocket thought, as Harry Abensour rose upon the admiral's furtive glance.

"Rufus," prompted Abensour as he flicked through some papers and glossy photos in a manila folder, "we thus come to a second item on our agenda, per Admiral Burke. Miss Mae Tanaka, who hypothetically *may* be an operative of the Central Intelligence Agency, has helped confirm certain incidents, occurring immediately after the death in Tokyo of *Yakuza* Boss Hama, aka Colonel Akira Matsumoto—'The Butcher of Rangoon'—and recovery of an artifact which hypothetically might be called the Korean Jade Dragon…"

Something didn't smell right. He definitely sounded like a prosecutor on Rocket's favorite radio program, "The Amazing Mr. Malone."

"You know I'm not at liberty to discuss such a thing," protested Rocket, "even if I were to know about such a thing…*sir.*"

"Funny you should mention the word 'liberty,'" prodded Abensour. "Because the incident in question involves your liberty *after* the death of Boss Hama. Do you recall an establishment in San Francisco's Chinatown, on Sacramento Street, known as the 'Half Moon Palace?'"

It was as if a sword stabbed the back of Rocket's chair and ripped through his viscera.

"I-I'm not clear," fumbled Rocket, "what's this got to do with my flight over Shanghai, sir?"

"Dammit, son!" pounded Captain Connor. "It was a chink cathouse!" The old man looked to Admiral Burke. "So your fella from ONI here claims my fella burned it to the ground?"

Admiral Burke nodded, gesturing to Abensour. "Continue, Harry."

"The Half Moon Palace, Rufus...the truth."

Chafing at his collar, Rocket looked up at Abensour and admitted in a monotone, "I told you about the ChiCom POW in confidence, Commander Abensour. Like in a confessional."

"I'm not a priest, and though my uncle is a rabbi, I don't owe you any such courtesy. We are at war. Any asset that helps us win it is fair game. So...look into my eyes and answer me." Abensour walked around to Rocket's chair, hovered above and stared down. "You set fire to that brothel. Tell me why, on the record, such as it is."

Rocket didn't even raise his head. He wasn't going to tell these ofays.

And in that instant he was no longer stuck in an uncomfortable metal chair on the carrier, nor was the setting sun playing little flames upon the waves.

Instead, Rocket was on special leave to ONI and CIA in Pusan, in the besieged Republic of Korea, and face-to-face with a Chinese POW in grimy prison togs. The man's name was Li, an officer.

Li outlined the antiaircraft batteries protecting the Sui-jong bridges not because he'd renounced communism; rather, he just hated North Koreans.

But he shared one other motivation with the one person besides all of those cracker officers and sinister spies who'd interrogated him. One person who wasn't white, who was an outsider—whom he felt could empathize.

He confided in Rocket that his family had defaulted on debts to the wrong people—the worst people—and his wife and sister were the collateral, carried away to Canton, which the Chinese called Guangzhou, and from there to Hong Kong, then to Frisco.

To be used. To be used up.

And every sailor, Marine and vice cop on the take knew where all of that fresh meat ended up: the Half Moon.

Rocket never promised this man a damn thing. But he was going to be in Frisco anyway, as compensation for solving the Jade Dragon mystery. Bonelip Broussard was recovering from his wounds back in Tokyo, compliments of Boss Hama's *sumo* wrestler goons. What was the harm flying solo? He did it in the sky, why not in Chinatown? Call him a sucker for a sob story, even from a Commie stoolie.

There on the flag bridge of the Goodtime Dickie, Rocket saw himself checking in with the madam of the Half Moon Palace. The *real* madam, not the over-painted middle aged floozy who fronted the place as a dancehall serving soda pop and wontons.

The old bat smoked self-rolled cigarettes and had no teeth, and she mumbled in pidgin about choosing a "pretty lotus."

He told her his tastes were on the margins: either very young virgins, or girls who were already broken in from boyfriends or husbands back home. Moreover, his flavor was Cantonese, because those girls likely had experience with foreigners.

Nevertheless, Rocket figured that despite his officer's dress blues, necktie and white combination cap, he was still a nigger, so the house would send two less than fragrant lotuses.

Indeed when the muscled-up pimp arrived in the gaudy room served only by a Murphy bed, the two hookers he delivered were barefoot. One looked to be barley in her teens and was bawling; the other made no sound and her eyes were glazed-over. They were half-dressed in five-and-dime peignoirs.

Neither spoke anything close to English, so in his best Chinese Rocket asked, "*Ni zhidao Li Wu? Ta shi zai jiefanggjun duizhang, zai hanguo paishe do...*"

The name Li Wu made the teen's eyes widen. She pointed to the lolling, barely conscious woman. Rocket couldn't understand all of her rapid, stream-of-consciousness yammer but caught two repeated words. *Meimei.* Sister. And *shengbing.* Sick. Her sister, or Li Wu's?

Yet before he could get the teen to calm down and clarify, the other woman collapsed and planted her face right into the rickety Murphy bed's mattress, moaning.

Rocket and the teen flipped her over.

Foam bubbled over her lips. Her eyes had rolled up into their sockets. Her body went into full spasms. Holding her down, Rocket noticed the welts over veins in her arm. Then, as her legs jerked involuntarily, he saw reddened pin-pricks dotting the top of her left foot.

He'd seen needle marks that bad in Chicago, among

the junkies infesting the north side beatnik beats, and in Harlem, through Bonelip's Jazz comrade and sometime gangster, Patten Leather Mackey. But he'd never witnessed anyone this sick from heroin before.

Suddenly the woman heaved so violently she almost threw Rocket off the bed. And just as quickly, she went limp under his grasp. No breath, no pulse.

"Rufus…?"

Abensour's voice tugged Rocket from gauzy, melted memories back to the sharp angles of the flag bridge.

"The question stands, Rufus. The Half Moon Palace—something bad happened in there, right? Something you saw…before you set the place ablaze?"

Rocket finally locked eyes with Abensour and said, "Negative, sir. I do not recall an incident other than a conflagration of unknown origin, which I witnessed from the street. I gave testimony to the police and the fire marshals, none of whom were impressed with the fact that I was a Naval officer. Rather, I was a *nigger* at the scene of a fire."

And that fire sure did burned fast, thanks to kerosene that the pimps were using to fuel a single meager heater in a caged pen lined with mattresses.

Over a dozen women clung together inside the cage. They had buckets for washing and cheap perfume and talc when the washing didn't take.

Rocket broke the old toothless madam's arm to get her to cough up the cage's location. Once in this labyrinthine cellar, *jujitsu* learned in *Michiko-san's* tea house dispatched the pimp guards.

One of the guards was carrying a ballpene hammer as a weapon; now it was Rocket's and smeared with this hooligan's blood.

The sight of a black man in a black uniform wielding

a bloody hammer might have unnerved the captives, but when they saw the quivering teen clutching his arm, they seemed to know he was neither a john nor a tormentor.

Rocket shouted in Chinese that he was a friend of Li Wu, and asked about Li's wife. He didn't tell them about Li's poor sister, who remained upstairs. Through the steel wire of the cage, he saw one young woman sink her head, then lift it, eyes wet. She pantomimed a cut-throat gesture and sank her head again.

Enraged by the revelation, Rocket smashed the cage lock with the hammer. The captives rushed out of their pen, still hugging one another. Abruptly they stopped, fretted, and looked to him to order the next move. After all, this place wasn't a pleasure palace. It was a prison, designed to keep them in.

And, it was something else.

Rocket shifted his attention on a long steel table, like the ones on a ship's sick bay. It was stacked with tin steel cups, and what looked like trays of glass syringes. He was immediately transfixed by the baked-on umber residue in each cup. Beside the cups lay the syringe needles—doubtless spent ones, as they were strewn among cotton swabs flecked with dried blood.

The teen he'd rescued gestured toward small Buddha statues stacked on shelves beyond the table. That's when Rocket understood what was going on. This was way beyond what the *goombahs* in New York or the beatnik pusher-men in Chicago were peddling, he thought. And these cats were trying out their recipe on their own sex-slaves, as guinea pigs!

"Ladies, we're airing outta this evil spot, fast. But first…"

Rocket grabbed the small heater and carried it to a few open crates stuffed with straw. There were more

Buddhas inside them. It was then he saw a piece of canvas which had lined one of the crates. It was lettered with Chinese characters he'd never seen before. And a flower stamp, in purple ink.

An orchid.

Rocket wet the crate's straw with kerosene from the heater. Zippos were a dime a dozen at Woolworth's, so once Rocket pushed the last half-naked girl up through a basement window he'd busted out, he flicked up a flame and tossed the lighter onto the crates.

Thanks to the tightest of lips in Chinatown, the only mention of the fire was a back-page photo in the *Chronicle*. It was Rocket flashing his trademark pearly whites. The caption read: *Negro Flyer saves Dancers from Ballroom Blaze*.

Yet even back-page photos could ride the bamboo telegraph. All the way back to Shanghai, for hopeful eyes to see. And for evil eyes to dissect...

Rocket blinked his own eyes, saw he was back in his chair onboard the *Bonhomme Richard*, with only an instant passing.

"Have you heard of an outfit called a tong or 'triad?'" pressed Abensour.

"No sir."

"Well they've heard of you, according to our information. Any idea why?"

"Fans of my aerial exploits, sir?" Rocket grinned, seemingly composed and impertinent.

"*Can it*, mister!" groused Admiral Burke. He looked to the skipper, then to Abensour. "This kid's getting on my nerves. Wrap it up."

"With all respect, sirs," offered Rocket with abrupt gravity. "All I will say about Frisco, and this fire is..." Rocket gestured to his own face, then showed the rich tea pigment on the top of his hands. "…I'm not someone who thinks slavery is a-ok. The girls working in there weren't mere dancehall dames. They weren't even human beings. They were cattle."

Harry Abensour slid back in his chair and shot back, "Noted. And so what are your thoughts on the stateside heroin rackets?"

"I don't know a thing about dope, smack; whatever they call it these days, sir."

"Ah, yet you know enough to call it by its New York aliases. You holding out on me? There wouldn't be any dope peddlers among the fans of your 'aerial exploits,' eh, Rufus?"

Captain Connor watched the sinew on Rocket's brown neck cord and pulse; he could tell his ace was going to blow.

"Lt. Crockett!" called Captain Connor, prompting Rocket to jump from his seat to attention. "Dismissed. Get outta here."

As Abensour gave a sly and inexplicable grin, Rocket snapped a salute to the panel, whipped a turn, and was escorted off the flag bridge by the X.O.

"Not a word to your squadron while we deliberate," Commander Hollins said, with solemnity rather than spite. "Wait for us to call you back in. One way or another, you and Seaman Broussard are going to be off this ship, temporarily…or permanently."

Rocket saluted, eager to drive the memory of the blaze from his brain with the bottle of *saki* stashed in his quarters. But before Hollins closed the hatch, Rocket heard Connor's voice. The old man never could give a proper whisper.

"*Orchids?*" Rocket heard the skipper grumble to Admiral Burke. "Is your Jew, here, yanking my pecker,

Arleigh?"

Chapter 5

Good-Bye, Praline Pie

"Bonelip" Broussard—meriney, green-eyed, squat and sweating—met his knight at the bulkhead hatch leading to the aviator's wardroom.

Not quite ripped but slightly torn by swigs of *saki*, Rocket pulled off his garrison cap adorned with its double silver bars and gold aviator pin, folded it into his web belt.

"Well, my faithful Sancho Panza," slurred Rocket, now unknotting and yanking off his tie, "gw'on and hit me with the 'I told you so's."

Rubbing the filé powder and thyme from his stubby hands onto his apron, Bonelip sighed and said, "Whatchew gwine say—dat you Bojangles Robinson-ed yo'self outta a ass-whuppin' from the Navy? *C'est vrai*. Whatchew did wid dem Marine flyboys, that'd get ya forgiven. Maybe even a passel more medals an' commendations. But dere's somethin' else y'all ain't telling me."

"I'm smelling gumbo. Let's go."

"Nah-unh. Gumbo'll keep. If dem white boys ate it up, I'll grill ya a cheeseburger. Now I'm gwine hip ya some true."

Rocket was head and shoulders taller than his squire and sidekick, but he always listened when Bonelip laid it down. And Bonelip sure did. Straight. No seltzer, no ice—

"Dig dis, daddy. I could be makin' paper playin' trombone fo' niggas in da Treme an' white tourists out on Boi-bon Street. After dem *sumo* of Boss Hama sent my redbone ass to da hospital fo' three weeks I coulda had my ticket punched an' be home wid my fam'bly an' my music right now, jack. But y'all was too busy bein' a hero, an' so I re-upped fo' *yo'ass*."

"Where'd I be without, you, my friend, eh?"

"Keep sayin' dat. But now…now y'all getting' too biggity fo' yo' draws. We got *sloppy* wid dem leaflets and dat caper. We got *caught*. Dat's a omen, *frère*. "

Rocket shrugged. "I just want the folks back home catching hell every day, bowing, scraping, barely a dollar…I want them to have something to cheer about, man."

"Nah boss, some-*one* ta cheer. I hear ya, but it can't always 'bout 'Rocket,' 'kay?"

A few sailors in their dungarees pushed by, heading aft. Bonelip waited for them to pass, as they always stared when he and Rocket talked. Fraternizing, they always warned.

"Y'all never tole me what happened in Frisco," insisted Bonelip. "Is that why y'all wanna the hook-up wid Patten Leather Mackey up in Harlem—how y'all might need to talk 'bout what happened in dat chink ho' house?" The squire shook his head, sighed again. "Damn you, Rocket…"

Marcus Garvey Mackey, despite his regal name, ran Smack for Charlie "Lucky" Luciano and Meyer Lansky while fronting as a legit music promoter uptown back in the day. Word was he had some epiphany and retired to deal cards, poetry and a little reefer. Yet if anything was going on in the dope rackets, he'd know. Especially if the

Chinese were positioning to muscle-in on the Italians on either coast.

Bonelip pointed a finger at Rocket. "Foist of all, we ain't been straight wid one another, man. Y'all gotta trust me if we gwine make through dis war. Dat includes whateva mess you been in stateside. I ain't stupid like dese here white officers. It's about *heroin*, tell me true."

Rocket's mien changed. He slouched, tired and troubled, then doubled over as if an invisible wrecking ball slammed him in the gut.

"You a sage cat, daddy-o," whispered Rocket as he patted his sidekick on his beefy shoulder. "Yeah, smack. Pounds of it; the likes of which Mackey—or no one else—has ever seen. I kept it off the streets. I saved a bunch of women from the streets." Then Rocket expelled a heavy, sad breath. "I didn't save the two women I'd promised I'd save. But I saved enough…"

"Boss—"

"Nah, listen. That mess in Frisco…it's like I was watching myself do good, not actually doing good. My *real* self, oh man, I dunno, Bonelip. That real self had the audacity to ask them boys at Osan if they wanted my autograph…and of course here I go gonna sell Ted Williams' as a stake on a card game. Ain't I a piece of work? I'm here for all the wrong reasons, man."

"I think I understand now," smiled Bonelip. "Look go set down ta eat. Food'll ease yo' mind."

*****

A few other officers had slurped the remaining gumbo and were now sopping up the remainder with slices of buttered white bread.

Rocket walked in, and took a chair at the green felt-topped table. The others in their short-sleeved service khakis had been speculating all through dinner why Admiral Burke himself had motored over from the *St. Paul.*

A spindly colored messboy named Carl popped over to Rocket's side and said, "No gumbo left, Lieutenant. But I'm about to bring out some a Mr. Broussard's praline pie and ice cream."

"Its okay. Got a cheeseburger coming."

"Cheeseburger?" snapped Ensign F. Grayson Morse, Jr., one of Leiffer's toadies, fresh from Annapolis and even fresher from flying school at Patuxent Naval Air Station in Maryland. "Sorry we ate up your swamp stew."

Cool as a fan, Rocket reminded himself. *Don't let him gin you up…*

Morse smirked. "Chatter is you had a little woodshed moment up in the tower. Something a colored movie star like you isn't used to, huh?"

Lt. St. Anselmo, seated at table, tried to detoxify Morse's venom, joking, "He's the colored Kirk Douglas."

Lt. Webb added, "Nah, he's Marlon Brando. *Viva Zapata*! Oscar-winner!"

"Brando isn't colored," snickered Lt. Zwicky, elbowing. "He's Italian."

"Same thing," cracked Webb.

"Hey…watch it, *boombotz*," shot St. Anselmo, with fake outrage.

Rocket chuckled then tilted his head to Carl.

"Check on my burger. Slap some fried potatoes on the plate. Oh and bring the whole pie and the tub of ice cream to me, directly. I want to slice some for Mister Morse, here."

"Now we're talking, huh, hot-shot?" crowed Morse, as if he won.

"Yeah now we're cookin' with gas, Mr. Morse. Seeing that you are about to fly your first combat mission…and cease being a tailhook virgin…you get the big piece."

The rest of the men laughed. Morse did not.

"Did ya know I met Ted Williams?" offered Rocket.

"'Saved the ass of,' is more like it," clarified St. Anselmo with a laugh. "Though as a Cleveland Indians fan and someone doesn't much like Marines, I got mixed emotions!"

"Big deal," scoffed Morse. "My father, F. Grayson Morse, Sr., who is chairman of the most powerful committee in the House *and* personal friend of Senator Joseph McCarthy, a *true* American hero, has box seats to all the Senators' games in Washington."

"Do tell?" shrugged Rocket.

"Yeah! So we have dinner with ball players all the time, including Williams. Matter fact, we dined with Bob Feller *and* Yogi Berra the day before I got my orders to come to this floating coyote pack with you mangy animals."

Webb howled a canine protest as they awaited their dessert.

But Morse wasn't finished. "Saaaay," oozed the ensign, growing a slick, mean grin, "Griffith Stadium's right down the street from your colored college, right? That place teaches what—sewing? Auto repair?" Morse then gestured to his fellow flyers around the table. "These people need to learn useful trades, see, so they won't be on the dole or shuffling around or sticking up shoe stores or pumping out babies. I mean, come on!"

Carl brought out a metal tray of pie, ice cream and dishes. Bonelip followed him out, setting down Rocket's sizzling cheeseburger. Bonelip quickly noticed the muscles in Rocket's neck tightening. Something was going to pop off, soon.

"Yes Mr. Morse," smiled Rocket, hiding his fierce desire to slap this ofay fool. "Howard University. 1950. Engineering major. Minored in Classical Romance Literature, not car repair."

"Come on Rocket," groaned Zwicky. "Football and dames, not books, was your rice bowl. I'll have you know, Ensign Morse, that Mr. Crockett here was a star halfback in college. What were you—a towel boy for the Middies in the Army game? Ha!"

"I was a trainer *and* manager for the team, Mr. Zwicky," Morse fired back, after jabbing his tongue in his cheek. "And I captained my sailing crew to a trophy. That's different than being like a circus novelty. I mean... doesn't it bother you, Zwicky—"

"That's 'Mister,' or 'Lieutenant,' kid..."

"Hmmm...okay, doesn't it bother *any* of you that things that would get you or I busted, they let slide with *him* because they're afraid of Eleanor Roosevelt and the pinkos and pansies controlling the NAACP?"

Zwicky just shrugged. Yet Rocket's phony cheese was still stitched on his face, the envy of any minstrel's.

"Pie, Mr. St. Anselmo," offered Rocket, cheerily and with a servant's affectation. "Mr. Webb? Mr. Zwicky? I'll even save some for Leiffer. And the biggest piece of praline pie for you, Mr. Morse."

"*Rock*-et..." Bonelip moaned through taut lips. He dipped and whispered, rapid fire, "...we gots problems, now you wanna move up ta trouble?"

"One scoop of ice cream for y'all, but two for Mr. Morse."

"I know you're a bunko artist, Crockett," sniped Morse, awaiting his sweets, "so secure the fake coon act."

"Coon? Lil' ol' me?"

Rocket's act was having its desired effect.

"I've got your number, pal! And I can send a cable straight to my dad, who'll phone Senator McCarthy and you and everyone around you are *done*."

"Come on, kid," cautioned Webb. "You're my new wingman so don't make me despise you, copy?"

"Might wanna listen, Mr. Morse," chimed Rocket as he scooped up two fluffy mounds of vanilla and dropped them onto the plate next to a massive wedge of pie. Rocket cocked his head at the two white lumps. Morse snatched the plate away and dug in.

"Bad enough," mumbled the ensign, mouth full, "that I have to eat with you…now I have to bear you staring at me while I eat?"

"No, just thinking. That brunette dame in the mink, at Yokosuka in May…came to see you off. Fiancée, right? Susan?"

The other men pulled back from the tabletop, wisely. But Bonelip edged in under the guise of refilling coffee mugs.

"*Rock*-et…" came the sidekick's faint warning.

Morse hissed, "*Suzette*, not Susan. Her parents flew her to Japan to say goodbye to me."

"Ah, but she goes by 'Rose' as a nickname," baited Rocket.

"How the hell'd you know that out?" seethed Morse, squeezing his linen napkin as if it was Rocket's throat.

"She went to a women's college in ole Virginny, right Morse?"

Morse stabbed his wedge of praline pie with his spoon as a crud of spittle and ice cream tumbled from his mouth. "Don't cross me, nigger…"

"…but she told me it was down at some redneck

tattoo shop in Roanoke where she got that tiny red rose on her right…nah …her left breast. I yeah, if I recall…"

Before Morse could jump and swing, Rocket kicked his chair from under him, spilling the young hothead forward. Rocket yanked Morse's forearm around to his scapula, then pinned him on the felt table top.

"You'll be Portsmouth… in irons nigger!" coughed Morse, in excruciating pain. "And hung in your cell!"

Morse's squirming was no match for Rocket's steel sinew. "The rest of you fellas concur with Ensign Morse? Speak now, or forever hold your piece. Just like 'Rose' held my piece in Tokyo…"

"Damn it, Rocket!" protested Zwicky. "You aren't making this easy for us."

Crushing Morse tighter, Rocket snorted, "Nah it's always about making things easy for all of you. Not tonight. Not before I say good-bye on liberty…" He shoved his knee into Morse's rear end and Morse let out a squeak. "Yeah you son of a bitch, *liberty*. Not the brig. So I ask …it was Mr. Morse who spilled this ice cream, right? *Right?*"

Quickly, St. Anselmo nodded, then Webb.

Zwicky cursed and bolted to the couch on the bulkhead. "Okay! Let the bastard go for chrissakes," he said. Then he added, "Morse, jeez…you did this to yourself!"

Bonelip called nervously, "Rocket…let de young fella go. Lawd y'all don' need dis."

Putting his lips close to Morse's reddening ear, Rocket whispered, "Don't you ever screw with me again, little boy. Now…I'm gonna let you up. Carl will fetch a sponge, no worries. And we'll pretend this never happened. These aviators are going to vouch for me. Not because they like me. It's because they *don't* like you."

It was a few minutes before Lt. Commander Leiffer arrived with two more Sea Knights, Malone and Duquesne, who were in their flight suits and leather jackets. They'd just come in from patrol, craving fresh coffee from the Proctor-Silex.

"Mr. Morse made a mess," explained St. Anselmo. "Rocket's helping him clean it up."

"Get a grip on yourself, Morse," droned Leiffer. "As for you, Crockett, guess what? Chopper to Nagasaki lifts off at 0930 tomorrow. You are to be packed and standing-to on the flight deck at 0900. You too, Broussard. No silverware in your duffle."

"I ain't planning to eat with no Navy spoons during my liberty, sir."

Leiffer pulled a blue envelope out of his back pocket and tossed it onto the green felt table. Rocket opened it, fingered the contents.

"Draft for fifty dollars for you," huffed Leiffer with a heap of disdain. taste of disdain. "Twenty dollars for Broussard. Two commercial tickets from Hawaii once you clear Subic Bay. Pullman vouchers for the Central Pacific from San Francisco to Chicago. Bus vouchers for anywhere else you two want to go."

Fifty bucks? Rocket had twin rolls of fifties hidden in his rack's thin mattress.

Pocketing the bounty, Rocket thanked Leiffer with mock graciousness, sending the C.O. to the Proctor-Silex shaking his head. Rocket picked up his cheeseburger, took a lion's bite and smiled as he chewed.

"See ya in a month, fellas," said Rocket, his cheeks bulging as Morse sat quaking and florid—in silence.

Bonelip placed his hand on his knight's heaving and muscled back. "Um, I think its best if y'all just get some sleep. I'll clean up down here." He faced Malone and

Duquesne. "Cheesburgers, sirs?"

*****

That night, as he dreamed of Brenda, he had visitors to his quarters. It wasn't like the visitors he'd received upon joining the Navy—urinating on his rack, pouring bleach on his dress blues, threatening him with hot laundry irons or leaving torn-out magazine shots of apes and baboons taped over photos of Viola Jean and the good Reverend Samson Crockett, Sr.

Rather, the visitors left a piece of paper stuck in the hinge of the hatch to his quarters, with the words: *Rocket Crockett, He's our man. If he can't do it, No one can.*

It was signed Mario St. Anselmo, Dick Webb, Ted Zwicky, P.J. Malone, Bart Duquesne. Strike Squadron 25, Sea Knights. Morse's signature was absent.

Rocket never saw it, as someone had snatched it way by the time Bonelip roused Rocket for breakfast at 0630.

And so Rocket departed the carrier with bitterness, apprehensive. Not the best way to say good-bye and start a three week liberty that was both reward… and punishment.

CHAPTER 6

FIRST THING SMOKIN'...

"Woo-wee, lawd," harped Bonelip as he scanned the sports page, at the Pullman's open berth window. In his blindingly white summer dress blouse and bell-bottoms, he looked like he'd dropped out of a human-sized Cracker Jack box. "Brooklyn dropped a doubleheader to dem Phillies…Giants beat da Cardinals. I'm tellin' ya, don't count Mays out."

Rocket wasn't listening. He sat neat in his service dress khaki, but pensive, for his eyes were tracking a target from behind his Ray-Bans…

There he was again, Rocket noted—a man. Brown sharkskin blazer, and porkpie hat, strolling in and out of the station doors. Unclear whether he was Korean or Chinese, but he was definitely not Japanese.

The conductor at the tiled and Spanish-adobe San Jose Station blew his whistle. The red-capped porters sweated like Hercules to bring the white gloved passengers' steamer trucks and suitcases to the platform.

"Boss…*boss?*" prodded Bonelip, crinkling and lowering his newspaper.

"Remember I said someone was ghosting us?"

"Uh-huh," sighed Bonelip, anxious to shove off and sample the dining car's fare without fear of Jim Crow.

"Well he's here, my faithful Sancho Panza."

It was the same guy who'd flown 3,000 miles in

the same Pam Am seaplane out of Pearl Harbor to San Francisco Bay, back row, window, second level.

"Then by bus to here," explained Rocket deduced, peering at his squire over his sunglasses. "And he ain't got no luggage…see?"

"Hmph," huffed Bonelip incredulously, "He oriental and got on at Pearl? Come on, *frère*, y'all know how many Chinese, Japs whatever what lib in Hawaii. And we know dem niggas loves to gamble. Prob'ly blown his whole pineapple rent to fly here an' catch the first thing smokin' to Reno so's he can toss dice and play stud poker."

"Stay on your game, regardless," directed Rocket, turning his Ray Ban-shaded gaze back to the slowly emptying platform.

The horn of the bullet-like, red-visaged diesel locomotive blared twice. The conductor hollered, "*All aboard!*"

Finally, the San Jose station loudspeaker crackled with another voice in that cadence and melody only heard when the thrill of the rails beckoned:

"Ticketholders only! The California Zephyr… making stops at Sack-ree-mento…Reno…Salt Lake City…Denver…Ohhh-maha and Union Station Chicago, with continuing Pennsylvania Railroad service to Indianapolis, Cincinatt-ah, Charlottesville-Virginia, Washington, D.C., Balt-tee-more, Philadelphia… arriving Pennsylvania Station New York City! *Alllll-aboooooooard!*"

The stranger reappeared, butted out his cigarette in an ashbin and sprinted to the platform. Rocket craned his neck to watch the man board one of the second class cars beyond the ultra-futuristic stainless steel "bubble dome" observation car.

"He's on the train," muttered Rocket as the metal beast lurched forward, then slowly built momentum, until the station and platforms were a memory.

Instead of washing for dinner, Rocket sloughed his shoulderboard jacket, slipped off his brown shoes—as the Navy blessed only its aviators with the right to wear brown—then folded down one of the compartment's bench seats to form a bed.

The crisp sheets embroidered with the Central Pacific's monogram already wrapped the mattress cushion.

The porter, so very happy to see not only Negro servicemen, but an officer—a flyer at that—dropped off extra hot towels and a fruit and candy basket liberated from the service car. Usually, such treats were delivered by comely chicks called Zephyr Girls in Hawaiian or Cowgirl garb. But not to passengers like Rocket and Bonelip.

"We stan' out like raisins in a rice bowl on dis here trip," said Bonelip to the porter as he peeled off a ten spot. "So y'all take care a us."

Motioning for a steamy towel from Bonelip, Rocket stripped down to his tank top skivvy, swung his legs onto the bed and exhaled loudly, as if all of the war and death and artifice tainting his adventures were expelled in that single breath.

Bonelip lay the towel across Rocket's face.

"Got some bumps under yo' neck, boss," said Bonelip, almost tenderly. "Lemme shave you next time."

All Rocket could muster was a noise of weariness.

"I'm axe-ally gwine see if dem porters can scare up some whales on dis trip. Get in some cards. Cool?"

"Nah, low profile," came the muffled voice from under the towel.

Viola Jean's brother—Rocket's Uncle Alonzo—had been a Pullman man on the New York Central. He'd formed the Brotherhood with A. Phillip Randolph, struck for colored men's rights and even threatened ole FDR into defying the Dixiecrats and passing the first fair employment rules during the war. For that, the bigshots declared him a Red, and he resigned from the union rather than bring heat on Randolph.

Rocket recalled the afternoon before Alonzo drove him to the depot to catch the bus east for flight school at Patuxent. The good Reverened Samson, Sr. had declined to see Rocket off, for he'd already lost his dear Sammy.

As they waited in the car during that Tennessee downpour, Uncle Alonzo told Rocket about the time, quite by chance, he'd met Sammy on the Santa Fe Southern line. Sammy had been on his way from Tuskegee to McGuire Field in New Jersey, 1943, to handle the old P-41s. He had to sit in the dingy, Spartan colored section all the way to Washington, D.C. despite being an officer and a pilot.

Once Alonzo saw it was indeed his nephew in that jazzy uniform, he snuck him goodies the white folks had for dessert, scented towels and soap, magazines—all of which Sammy promptly shared with the other Negro passengers.

And Alonzo hipped him to the places he should stay onboard, rather than stretch his legs. The local crackers didn't like uppities wearing officer uniforms and talking like proper white men as Sammy had learned to do at Oberlin College.

Uncle Alonzo's affirmation was now swimming in Rocket's head.

"Things'll be better in the jet age for us, Rufus," he'd sworn. "Forget your daddy's sermons about turning cheeks and quiet dignity. Have pride in your noggin, fire in your belly." Then he laughed and added, "But don't showboat. Don't give these snowflakes a *reason* to mess with you, because they sure feel they got a *right* to do so, ya hear?"

Alonzo was now living in the fruit cellar of Rocket's parents' house, so said the last telegram from Memphis. He'd taken to whiskey and dames as tonic for his fall without a net.

Drifting, dreaming, Rocket saw his uncle and Sammy again. They told him he'd be safer if he'd just leave those girls cowering in the Half Moon waiting to be raped or shot-up with dope, or both. He saw himself in the Typewriter's cockpit, waiting for the go sign from the deck master, steam rising from the catapult. The sky was his only sanctuary. Yet the go sign never came, and he was trapped.

A knock on the compartment door roused him. Bonelip wouldn't knock; a conductor would announce himself. He threw off the towel, now clammy.

It was already dark. How long had he been out? Rocket heard the door handle jiggle, and then a second sound Rocket recognized—the lock was being picked.

Gingerly, Rocket swung out of the bed, reaching for his canvas suitbag. Inside it was his .45. Even a colored officer had a right to carry that. But the clip was in Bonelip's duffle, by the door. That was the compromise for being a colored officer, ironically. No live rounds…

Rocket slid to the floor, silent. Crouching, he aimed the pistol with one hand, he reached for the latch with the other. Even an empty .45 was a scary sight when pointed at your groin.

With quick turn, Rocket yanked open the door. A man in a pork pie hat gasped as he tried to keep balance. The

Zephyr hit a curve just as Rocket hooked the interloper's legs. The combination of motion sent the man stumbling. Rocket pulled him inside the compartment and shut the door before strolling passengers could note the ruckus.

"Who the hell are you?" yelled Rocket, cocking the empty for show.

The man didn't wince or blink. He also smelled, not from an ocean of travel without a change of clothes, but from sweet spices Rocket had only smelled before in the restaurants of Pusan. He studied the man's face. No, definitely not Japanese… or Chinese.

"*Iyagi!*" barked Rocket in Korean. This cat had clearly stopped in Oakland's Koreatown for some home cooking and never brushed his teeth.

"Relax, pal," huffed the man, in perfect English. "And you might want to load that Colt, unless you're planning to hit me with it."

"On your knees!" Rocket barked, keeping up the bluff despite the realization that this cat was some sort of professional tough guy. "Hands on your head."

The man complied. Rocket, keeping the pistol leveled, kicked him in the gut.

The interloper doubled over with a groan. It gave Rocket time to dig into Bonelip's duffle, pop in the clip and pull the slide before the Korean could recover.

"Y-You bastard…I'm on your side…" coughed the intruder. "The name's Suh. Bert Suh. Check my I.D.; it's here in my wallet. I'm a private dick in L.A. Sometimes I contract-out."

"Oh yeah? To who?"

Chapter 7

...and the Last Man Alive

The Zephyr's late-supper white-linen dining car passengers got an eyeful: a colored Naval officer in dress khakis striding stone-faced with a Korean man in a pork pie hat. As he passed the slack-jawed stares, Rocket fingered the now *loaded* .45 in his jacket side pocket, pressing the muzzle to Suh's hip.

The middle of the train was demarcated by a futuristic domed-bubble observation car. The Zephyr had left the fertile valleys of central California and rolled into the notched mountain passes of the Sierras. The vista from the observation car was a less spectacular in darkness, but as the full moon bounced off the snow-capped peaks, the effect was both eerie and intoxicating.

A few passengers lounged in the swivel chairs, enjoying drinks and swaying their heads to piped in music by Les Brown & Ames Brothers, and Rosemary Clooney were piped in.

Still, no sight of Bonelip. Rocket was worried.

Suddenly a familiar voice—a dame's—purred, "These tunes aren't your jive, are they flyboy?"

One of the swivel chairs turned, languidly propelled by two legs in seamed nylons. Pert cherry lips wrapped around a straw plunged into what had to be sloe gin fizz. Mae's favorite.

"Miss Tanaka," said Rocket smiling wryly, "yeah...

some Lionel Hampton and a little Howlin' Wolf would be keen n' serene about now."

Sucking out the last of the tart cocktail, Mae Tanaka looked toward the bulge in Rocket's jacket pocket. "Packing more than one gun, I see. Hope you didn't hurt poor Bert."

After allowing Suh to sit, Rocket clicked the safety on the .45 then edged into an adjoining chair.

The last time he'd seen Mae, the Jade Dragon had been bagged, tagged and carted off to Lord knows where. She had been whisked away by her CIA bosses before the Jap *yakuza* and Commie agents discovered who she really was.

"Interesting fact…" offered Mae, "…this train passes by an internment camp in the state of Nevada. It was where my parents were forced to live during the war. Uncle Sam seized our grocery store, sold it for a few bucks to bigshots who razed it and are now unloading the lot for this freeway thing California's got planned. This is a pilgrimage, of sorts."

"Lucky I'm going your way, huh?"

"Have you told him anything, Bert?"

Suh shook his head. "Just that someone wanted to meet him."

"And here I thought Koreans and Japs hated each other," posed Rocket with a tinge of sarcasm.

Chuckling, Suh answered, "We're both Americans, pal. Not to mention, Uncle Sam pays me fifty bucks a day plus expenses on contract. I'm your guardian angel all the way from Honolulu to the Windy City."

From the far end of the car, Bonelip finally appeared, toting another gin fizz for Mae and a plate of deviled eggs for himself.

"Hey boss! So we all together again, huh? I figured

I'd let y'all sleep while I seized me some grub in de dining car. Baked sole wid rosemary. *Superbe*."

Bonelip kissed his fingers French style and sat. The sidekick carried his own Creole spice wherever he went; he sprinkled it on his late snack. Suh snatched an egg from under Bonelip's scowl.

"Boys, some privacy?" intoned Mae to the sidekicks.

After a nod from Rocket, Bonelip departed with Suh and the plate of eggs.

Alone with her suave guest at last, Mae declared, "Let's get this straight, flyboy. I'm over you. This is strictly business."

"You ain't my type anymore anyway," parried Rocket, sliding the lounge chair opposite her. "From now on my *yellow* gals are Fredi Washington or that Tarzan flick chick Dorothy Dandridge..."

"Not funny," huffed Mae huffed. She tapped a cigarette on the cocktail table. "Light me."

Rocket obliged with his Zippo. "Okay, okay. So gimme the straight skinny, sister—why are you really on this train?"

Mae exhaled a plume of peppery smoke and revealed, "CIA briefed Abensour at ONI last month that we are trying to infiltrate the top tongs in Hong Kong and the ones who escaped to Formosa." She took another puff then said, "Much to my disgust we've even cut deals with *Yakuza* bosses to get intell. Now flyboy, these tong characters make *Yakuza* look like the Three Stooges when it comes to organization...and longevity."

"Infiltrating gangs—that something for narko flatfoots, not spies. Or the U.S. Navy."

The Zephyr's public address previewed a 7a.m. stop at Yosemite for quick sight-seeing. Mae leaned in closer. "Hank Abensour was trying to gauge you. He had to be cryptic, as your skipper didn't have the clearance to hear half of what we know. We're worried that a possible war between the tongs and the Mob, the Outfit, whatever you want to call it, is brewing over the heroin rackets. This world is changing, and the vice and curse of choice in this atomic age is going to be narcotics."

"That I already surmised, babydoll. What's this got to do with me?"

"Their war will affect national security, even the course of the war with the Communists."

"Ain't enough junkies in the world to support *two* drug stores, one Chinese, one Italian," mulled Rocket. "Unless everyone turns into a Jazzhound or a beatnik. There's something more to this, right?"

The train shuddered as it reached a steeper grade. Jagged peaks glowed blue in the inky panorama.

Mae searched the majesty beyond the glass, found some courage. "Of all of the tongs in China, the Orchids are by far the most vicious. They operated opium dens as far back as the 1850's, then morphine around World War One. After that, they started running a little heroin. Like the other tongs, drugs were never their main rice bowl."

"I sense a 'however,' Mae…"

Mae swigged, rather than sipped her gin fizz. Something was fishy and Rocket didn't have a clothespin big enough for his nose. "*However*," said Mae with a sigh, "Uncle Sam and British MI-5…we sort of helped the Orchids…"

Rocket immediately understood. "Your bosses got them hooked on getting us all hooked."

Rocket swiveled away from her, toward the night sky above the dome.

"Rocket, sweetie… listen. It started when the Japanese invaded in 1937. And when the Reds decided cut loose from our direction fighting the Japanese, there were hotshots in the old O.S.S., and now in the CIA, who had the bright idea that running drugs could help the Kuomintang get a leg up on Mao. Little did they know the Orchids were already plugged in, before the commie takeover and after. They've got just as many friends in Peking as they do in Taipei and Hong Kong. They even use casinos in Macau to broker deals between two supposed enemies. So yes, *we* inadvertently helped create the heroin trade out of the East. The Mob, theirs is based in Turkey, Pakistan. Lab's are in Sicily, West Germany. That's the usually brown powder hip cats and junkie trumpeters shoot. This stuff is different. They call their product 'China White.' And one day, it's going to hit America like a tidal wave…"

Communists were freedom's gravest enemy—that's what the powers-that-be drummed into Rocket's brain. But dealing with Mae always muddied that notion, and now Rocket contemplated the fat cats and fanatics who'd sent him to war: men who shrugged off the Kluxers who murdered Sammy, who cackled that it was un-American to fight for a fair wage like Uncle Alonzo did…and who passed their torch onto young snakes like F. Grayson Morse, Jr.!

Mae rose and stepped to the back of Rocket's lounger. "Flyboy, in San Francisco, you did more damage to the Orchid Tong in one day than the FBI or the crime families in New York and Chicago have in five years!"

"Ha! Here's the rub, huh. That's why I'm now dead in the middle of this."

Mae jerked his chair around so she could face him. She dropped to her knees and tugged his sinewy shoulder. "Rocket, there is something ungodly about their leader, the so-called 'Dowager.' We don't know her real name.

Our intel says she's barely older than me, but it also says they speak as if she's always been married to the old dead boss, which is impossible."

"Why?

"Because he immigrated here after the Civil War."

"Lots of Chinese refugees came here when Mao took over."

"No. The *American* Civil War. To work on *this* very railroad. His name was David Chow. He moved back to China to run the Orchid Tong. Supposedly died there an old, old man."

"This is nuts," groused Rocket, still avoiding Mae's eyes.

"This woman, the Dowager—she rules from Shanghai."

That caught his attention more than the spook story about immortal chinamen. "Shanghai?"

"Uh-huh…which you bombed—with your handsome, 'dark Gable' face."

Drawing a deep, uneasy breath, Rocket said, "I rubbed her nose in it…"

"Yes," whispered Mae, edging closer and resting her finely-coiffed head on Rocket's arm. "The agency wants to erase the mistake of helping them grow their dope trade. It wants to flush them from the shadows, retrace their lines back to her. Kill the 'mother' root, and the rest will wither and die."

"And I'm the bait."

Rocket could feel her nod. "Abensour gave you to us again. But don't worry. Bert's good at his job and he'll be your back-up." Mae lifted her head. Sensing no resistance she slinked, high heels and all, onto Rocket's lap. "*Mama-san's* not going to let anything happen to you."

She offered her lips. He saw no reason, even now, to refuse them. They tasted as he remembered: cherry blossom. Yes, his type after all…

*****

"Gotta a light?" asked Bert Suh as the pines and cliffs of the pass moved past the open hatch of the freight car in the pre-dawn dark, and a rush of mountain air extinguished his match.

Bonelip obliged. Each sidekick had resigned themselves to where their principals would likely end up: with each other, entwined.

"Man," complained Bonelip after a puff on his own Camel, "dis woulda been my foist night in a fo'true, foist class Pullman. Sheeeeyit." He looked to Suh, who was leaning on the hatch, seemingly and similarly displaced. "Say dere—you make decent bread woikin' private dick stuff?"

"Whaddya call decent?" joked Suh, drawing on his cigarette. "It pays the rent, pays for my family back in Korea. They had a rough go. First the goddamn Japs pillage, suck the countryside dry like vampires. Then the Communists rip the country in half."

"Russkies jus' got dere foist, is all, outta Manchuria. Jus' like Truman and dem axed 'em to. Dey jus' doin' what dey do."

"What—are you pro-Commie or something, pal?"

"Down da Big Easy we tell things like they is, cuz. Like, I still see you woikin' wid Miz Tanaka as a passel strange, her bein' a Jap. I mean, she Nisei, but a Jap, none-da-less."

"Like I told Crockett, I'm not prejudiced when it comes to cash." He paused. "Speaking of bread—you want the cabbage or what?"

"Dat's why we da hell back here, ain't it? An' don't worry 'bout dem porters snoopin'.''

From a woman's round toiletry case, Suh lifted a small brown paper bag. Doubly strange, as Bonelip had confirmed Rocket's observation that Suh didn't have any luggage.

But Bonelip's apprehension was quelled by a prize wrapped in waxed paper within the bag: green and flirtatious buds of marijuana.

"Hawaiian reefer," boasted Suh, handing Bonelip the package. "Worth a grand down in New Orleans or New York. But in these hayseed burgs on this train line like Denver or Salt Lake or Omaha—they will pay triple."

"Salt Lake? I thought Mormons di'n't smoke?" asked Bonelip. He sat on a steamer trunk, his back to Suh, to inspect the herb in better light.

"They'll smoke this," quipped Suh, taking a final puff then butting out his cigarette.

The Zephyr's horn, the chug and pulse of a muscled diesel and the incoming wind made it difficult for Bonelip to hear.

"I dunno 'bout four hundred dollars," dickered Bonelip. "Only gots two c-notes on me."

"We can come to an arrangement," answered Suh.

"So Miz Tanaka set y'all on us back at Honolulu? Ya know, Rocket made y'all at Pearl foist, den the station. My boy a hawk like dat."

Suh didn't answer.

"Hey man?" Before he could turn, Bonelip heard a sound. One, despite the cacophy and din of the rumbling train, with which he was intimate: the distinctive click and slide of cold, sharp metal.

Instinctively he whipped around, holding the package

of marijuana as a shield, just in time to take the stab of Suh's long and lethal switchblade.

With the blade lodged and useless, Suh drove his shoulder into Bonelip's chest, hurling himself and the chef into some crates and luggage.

"I strangle gators, boy!" strained Bonelip, catching Suh's head in his fat, burly arm.

But Suh had moves of his own, and too late Bonelip remembered this Korean style was called *taekwondo*.

Bonelip was now a heap on the floor, and about to have his head stomped by a Florsheim shoe.

Suddenly, the car door jerked open and two Pullman porters and a freight clerk who'd heard the commotion came piling in. They were all colored.

Time for Suh to beat feet. Snatching his knife on the fly, he bulldozed the tangle of subduing arms and escaped.

One of the porters helped Bonelip to his feet and spied the brick of reefer.

"We don't need this trouble, man."

"Ain't about dis stuff," shouted a frantic Bonelip, "Jus' toss it. I gotta help Rocket!"

*****

At the edge of the bed, Mae pulled on her stockings and fastened them her garters. Rocket, clad only in skivvie boxers and dogtags dangling between his pectorals, poured her some *saki*, returned to the bed and curled around behind her. He eased down a strap of her slip.

"Unh-unh, flyboy," trilled Mae after taking the shotglass full of warm fire. "No extra innings. I gotta find Bert."

Undeterred, Rocket continued to slide the strap downward as he gently nibbled the nape of Mae's long pale neck.

"He knows where he can find you," whispered Rocket between kisses. "Double header."

"Hmmm," sighed Mae after a sip of *saki*. "Batter up."

Rocket abruptly released Mae and looked up at the compartment ceiling. The decorated box housing the vent fan creaked loudly—twice—yet didn't kick on.

"I don't want to be cooled off anyway," cooed Mae.

But then came another creak, and it wasn't from the heave and pull of the California Zephyr. Mae frowned.

Suddenly the berth window imploded, taking the sash and curtains with it. Suh tumbled onto the floor, having swung in, acrobat-like, from the outer skin of the Pullman car.

He righted himself and kicked Rocket into the small sink.

"Hey smoke!" exclaimed the oriental turncoat, now brandishing his silvery blade. "That's how it feels to get kicked. Two birds with one slice." Suh was sweating, eyes wild and fixed first on a cowering Mae. "Vengeance for my mother and sister for the rape and slavery you Japs heaped on them…and for stealing our Jade Dragon!" Then he turned to Rocket: "…and ten grand from the chinks shadowing you and cutting your throat!"

Back to the wall, Rocket motioned Mae to stay put with one hand and gestured to Suh with the other.

"Come on, man," panted Rocket. His muscles bugled to strike but his brain calculated restraint. "Cut *me*? Oh you *know* that ain't the deal. I bet they want my black ass alive. Not only won't they pay you, they will do to you what all the Nip Emporer's soldiers did your momma…"

Mae's jaw dropped at the taunt but still she froze,

awaiting Rocket's signal. It needed to come quick.

"You think I'm scared of them?" screamed Suh, spittle flying. "I'll just kill you two, jump the train at Yosemite and cable them the news: *Jap Femme Fatale and Negro kill each other in Reefer deal gone bust.*"

"What reefer?"

Knowing Bonelip was likely coming any second, Suh wildly lunged at Rocket. Rocket countered his move with a shift of his feet, then gave Suh a Joe Louis left hook before grabbing Suh's wrist with the right.

Still, the marauder's grip on the spiky blade was like iron, and both men grunted and puffed in a contest of muscle, even as they heard shouts outside the compartment door.

Mae ended the match by bashing Suh over the head with a table lamp base.

"Your pistol? " Mae shouted to Rocket, but it was safely stowed.

In that instant of pause, Suh, though stunned and bleeding, had enough sand to elbow Rocket in the chest and tear out of the compartment just as Bonelip, a white conductor and a number of black porters squeezed down the narrow passageway past frightened passengers in pajamas and nightgowns.

Rocket, barefoot and bare-chested, took off after Suh.

Suh reached the coupling between cars just as the rising sun warmed the mountain air. Another group was converging from the other car, so Rocket knew his quarry had no place to go but topside, again. Grabbing the cold metal rungs of the ladder riveted to the car's hull, Rocket went up after him.

As the granite cliffs nearly scraped first the left, then the right side of the swaying carriages, Rocket rushed atop one, then two, now three of them the toward the engine, heart crashing against his sternum. Each jerk along the tracks meant death, but somehow both men made it to the fuel car and locomotive.

Suh wheeled, swiping the blade at Rocket a wide-eyed engineer peered out of a rear port.

The train chugged over a flat grade and sped up toward the sharp bend preceding the Yosemite tourist stop. But first it had to traverse a trestle spanning the windy valley and river a thousand feet below.

The men wrestled though each turn or jerk of the car threatened to spill them to their deaths.

Finally Rocket was able to break Suh's hold on the knife and kick it away with his bare toes. Exhausted and defeated, Suh spit blood at him.

"You can't hide from The Mother Blossom!"

"No ten grand for you!" heaved Rocket as the train reached the bridge, "but I'll give you twenty if you change sides…along with a promise I won't kill you… and another that I'll get the Jade Dragon back to your people when the war ends!"

Suh snickered."Too late, spade flyboy! They already know where you're headed!"

"What?" The train jerked again, its horn blasting. "I'm going home, to Memphis!"

"Liar! You're going to Harlem. But you can't stop the next shipment, because it's already on its way there!"

"Dammit I don't know what you're talking about… but by God, Bert, I'm gonna be the last man alive up here." He beckoned Suh. "But since you say we're both already screwed…how 'bout it—one last dance?"

With an animal's howl, Suh charged, throwing Rocket to the edge of the carriage as the deep, foggy valley opened up to the sun. Rocket twisted, pivoted and sloughed Suh's arms.

Suh's eyes told Rocket maybe he would have taken that deal after all. But gravity and momentum exercised their options on his soul. Suh plunged into the valley, his screams echoing until there was no sound but the thump of the California Zephyr's engine.

CHAPTER 8

BROADWAY BOUND

The California Zephyr pulled into the brief sightseeing stop at Yosemite, and was met by shearling-clad, Stetston-topped sheriffs rather than cheery tour guides.

Two thousand miles to the east, the Big Luck Chop Suey House on West 126th Street and Broadway was already frying up lunch while the steam presses of the Big Luck Prime Laundry hissed next door.

Seen one chop suey house or laundry, seen them all. But inside these shops, invisible, unlucky people toiled. Invisible by choice. Unlucky because they owed the tongs a piece of their lives. The unluckiest owed the Shanghai She-Devil. Such was the bad luck of Big Luck.

That afternoon, the rusted blades of a table fan did nothing to ameliorate the post-Labor Day heat, yet the Formica counter and the few metal tables were still full of folks looking for cheap grub. A plate of shrimp or beef chop suey and an egg roll with duck sauce, or chicken chow mein and three spareribs. All $3.50. That was the whole menu, from lunch till three in the morning.

Larry Ma—sweating profusely under his fedora and wearing a white linen suit cleaned and pressed for free next door—took his usual reserved table. He fingered his pinkie ring as he eyed two slick-haired white men wearing silk cabana shirts and alligator shoes.

Uncle Ri brought him a plate of shrimp chop suey—

the good shrimp, brought from the Fulton Fish Market via subway not an hour earlier—and a fork because Larry Ma abhorred anything traditional, even chop sticks.

"My pal Ri, you ol' *sei gwei!*" exhorted Larry called in mock magnanimity. He yanked Ri down by his stained apron, nodding toward the wiseguys and whispered, "If greaseballs come again you call. This is *our* corner, not theirs or *hak gwei* niggers."

"Y-Yes, Mr. Ma."

Between mock smiles and false small talk, Larry Ma added, "Package come here, soon. You keep in laundry, lock up. Leave out white powder starch for girls to come, they cut with starch. Then I come, I taste, you sell behind counter …"

"Y-Yes, Mr. Ma."

He patted Uncle Ri's head as if he was a pet. "Good. Julie proud, happy for you. You got something for me?"

Ri passed him an envelope under the table. Ma seemed perturbed. It was light. The two white men leaned in to see what was transpiring.

Ri offered his excuse, in Mandarin, and anyone who understood would have heard: "*I'm sorry, most beneficent Orchid Blockmaster Ma…but Broken Nose Feng of the Seven Dragon Tong, he came up from Canal Street and said we should pay him. I had to give him something or else—*"

"Broken Nose Feng no have Julie. I have Julie."

"B-But what if Broken Nose Feng comes back?"

Grinning his yellowed, broken teeth, Larry Ma removed a gold watch attached to a fob from his trouser pocket. "IRT come about now. You look. Make sure greaseballs look…"

Turning toward the smudged plate glass fronting the chop suey house, Ri fixed on the latticed ironwork of the viaduct carrying the subway over Broadway and the West Harlem ravine. The rumble of the train met his ears.

A body, bleeding and flailing, fell from the tracks as the train passed. Gasps in the restaurant joined screams and screeching car brakes outside. Even the two wiseguys took off to see who had splattered on the blistering pavement.

"Broken Nose Feng," chuckled Larry Ma. "He *drop in* for lunch, get it? Now he rice pancake. Get it…*flat!* Ha!"

With a shudder Uncle Ri pulled away from the window. *"He shi caineng zaijian dao wo xin'ai de nu'er?"* begged Ri. " She is my precious pearl."

Cool despite the commotion, Larry Ma said, "Daughter come back permanent when business start grow. Tiny problem in San Francisco getting solved, but you know, in America you got 'spend money to make money,' eh?" He stood, slapped Uncle Ri on the back. "Lata alligator," giggled Larry Ma. "You suppose say 'in while crocodile'."

*****

Mae's trip to the internment camp where Uncle Sam kept her family was postponed indefinitely as a result of Suh's attack. As was Bonelip's ticket south to the Big Easy, and, sadly, Rocket's sojourn home.

The Western Union booth outside D.C.'s Union Station held the wire from Viola Jean to her baby boy. Though heartsick, his mother conveyed that her sorority was having a picnic in his honor and even the white newspapers trumpeted his newest accomplishments over the East China Sea, though the pictures showed only Ted Williams flashing a thumbs-up. As for the Reverend

Samson Crockett, Sr.: nothing. The last line said: "Daddy needs more time."

He's had seven years…

Rocket stopped reading only to look up and watch Mae being led away to a black Packard by two white men dressed in suits as dark as the sedan despite the oppressive, swampy Washington heat. She blew a kiss as they shoved her into the car. Debriefing would be harsh.

The drab gray Navy Ford had already pulled away, with ONI tight-asses delivering a scolding from Commander Abensour.

"Proceed at your discretion," was the directive, ever cryptic. Proceed where? When Rocket left Pacific on this so-called liberty, he thought he was going back to his old room, his old bed hanging with airplane models crafted by he and Sammy. But the bait had to go where the fisherman wanted, because the worm never's able to read the mind of the guy with the line and pole. That line had always been cast east, to the Big Apple. And Rocket was almost there.

Rocket turned to search the station gallery, for he knew both the CIA and ONI, and maybe even g-men would put a tail on him. He counted two pairs of eyes on his back. Caucasian, and for the first time he was relieved by that notion.

Bonelip appeared, holding a chocolate ice cream cone that teetered and dripped perilously close to his fresh summer whites.

"Miz Tanaka down fo'da count, boss?"

"Uh-huh. She'll be ok, but we are on our own."

"Den we fixin' to get on a bus, plane or boosted jalopy an' get home?"

"Unh-unh," murmured Rocket, deep in thought."

Bonelip, exasperated, tossed the ice cream cone into

a garbage can, groaning, "Damn it, Rocket, bad enough we hadda come all de way hyah…now y'all wanna go where de bad guys want us? Herded, like hogs, to somewhere we don't even know? Why, boss, why?"

"To clean up a mess," muttered Rocket, almost inaudibly. "You can go to down New Orleans; I'll head to New York alone. Nothin' says you gotta help with every windmill, Sancho."

He stared at his sidekick. And after a few seconds of silence, Bonelip broke.

"Aw shucks, Rocket. Damn. Whachew need?"

Placing his hand gently on his squire's shoulder Rocket said, "Get the tickets for tomorrow afternoon. Now, see that hotel over there, on Massachusetts? Colored can get nice rooms there, especially if they're in the service. Book something cheap, wait for me…with the .45 *loaded*."

"Aye-aye, boss," sighed Bonelip. "Can I talk y'all outta dis *other* side trip?"

Rocket shook his head, but he did smile.

A taxi and streetcar ride later, Rocket arrived at a pleasant, sky-blue painted brick three story rowhouse topped by a spired cupola at 4th and T Streets, Northwest. He climbed the steps, and drew a deep breath…

It was a bittersweet trip, as Rocket had passed the Howard Theatre, site of many a jumpin' cabaret of big stars. He saw the Crystal Caverns—renamed Bohemian Caverns once he graduated. That spot was the site of many a date with many a girl inside its storied halls. But none of those girls was the girl he wanted.

That girl answered the door bell.

Even in high heels she was never taller than Rocket's lips. Even after a baby and raising a stepson her waist remained the same one he could grip to lift her in a dance or kiss. Still, she seemed more anchored, refined in string of pearls that matched her pearl earrings, her hot-ironed, conservative bob, subdued lipstick, flowered blouse, and pink apron.

"I asked you not to come," said Brenda LeBeau Goins through the screen door, arms folded.

Rocket could hear commotion inside: little boys, cheering. He searched over Brenda's petite shoulder and saw the dull white glow of a console television. He'd only seen a few in Tokyo that big.

Her stepson, Dr. Goins' seven-year-old, was reciting the narrative to the stirring theme of *The Adventures of Superman*; the two-year-old was doing his best to say "Truth, Justice and the American Way."

"In my Banshee I'm faster than a speeding bullet," joked Rocket. "No cape, though."

"It's the final installment of 'Superman and the Mole People,'" added Brenda, still with a little ice, though melting, left in her voice. "Even in a jet, you can't compete with the Mole People."

"I can't compete with a dentist, either."

"That was low," said the widow, iced fully and fingering her pearls. "I think you should go. I wouldn't want to divert you from danger and dye-haired chippies."

"Brenda…wait," pleaded Rocket. "I didn't even have a chance to see my parents or visit Sammy's grave. I have to go to New York. I coulda gone straight there from Chicago. But I came *this* way, to see *you*. You don't have to let me in…"

"Good, because the boys will get confused. Especially with the uniform." Brenda looked down, trying to battle back a smile. The ice receded and the smile won. "And you always look good in the uniform."

"I'm coming back…in my summer dress whites,

aviator badge and sword, white gloves. Just so you all can see it." Rocket paused, searching his brown dress shoes before pressing his hand to the door-framed mesh. "Even this screen's like seeing you in a dream. Maybe that's all I deserve."

Brenda opened the door.

Seeing her in the flesh—sharp, warm, real—made his eyes tear. His wet eyes prompted her's.

"I don't wanna to trouble your little fellas."

"Oh they are engrossed," sniffled Brenda. She blotted her own tears with the balls of her hands. "But you still can't come in. This must suffice." Then, thumbing away a wet track on his cheek, she whispered, "Rufus, it was so, so very…good…to see you."

Rocket swallowed hard, smiled and replaced his cap. "How're the Senators?"

"Worse than ever," laughed Brenda through her final tears. "A country boy named Mantle hit a homer that landed right on our roof. Even the lowly Detroit Tigers bombed the porch just last night."

Rocket whistled as he willed his eyes dry, "Wow, you got Mantle's ball?"

"Reporters tried to find it, never did."

"It'll turn up. Things always do." Rocket tipped his cap, backing down the steps. "Visiting the ole campus," explained Rocket, pointing to the library clocktower. "Well; I'm off."

Brenda nodded, smiling and waving, keeping more tears at bay.

Her stepson came to the door. She put her arm around him. "Who was that, Mommy? A Western Union man? More bad news, like when Daddy died?"

Brenda squeezed him to her hip, laughed. "No, sweetheart. He's a hero. But *bad* news to anybody who messes with him…"

*****

"Anything happen?" Rocket asked Bonelip as he stripped out of his dress service khakis. He unzipped his garment bag containing his other uniforms, and pulled out his tropical white service longs.

"Boss, why y'all wanna go in yo' Good Humor man outfit? Low key, remember?"

"Nah," answered Rocket, steadfast as he stepped into the white trousers and gestured Bonelip for the white short-sleeved shirt with the shoulder boards. "Hiding ain't the play no more, man."

"Uh-huh," mulled Bonelip, worried. "Windmill tiltin'. Well, telegram come in to da station. From ya boy Ralph DeWitt, prezdent of Smoov Mallard Hair Products. He hot ta talk to ya, man. Says it damn important."

"Ha! So we got a legit reason to go to New York after all," joked Rocket as he laced his spotless ivory shoes. But as he contemplated the implications of Bonelip's news, he frowned. What—he squirrely now after with the Navy pinched me for the Shanghai bit? Wanna cancel my endorsement deal before I've seen dollar one?"

"Dunno, *frère*," remarked Bonelip, as he traded ribbons and insignia from the service dress khaki jacket to the white shirt before draping it over Rocket's broad shoulders. "Want I should call him?"

"Not yet," pondered Rocket. "But use the roll of dimes on the dresser there. Make *four* toll calls. One, to ONI here in D.C. at the Navy Yard. Use Abensour's name. Tell them bastards we're going to New York, all right, and if the *kimchi* goes down, they better have our backs 'cause I'm done with the cloak and dagger mess."

"Gotcha," answered Bonelip, whisking Rocket with a clothing brush.

"Two," Rocket primped in the mirror, inspecting his mustache and the lay of his hair, "call my aunt in Brooklyn. Tell her we're coming to stay with her and she should tell the neighbors, Amsterdam News…the whole banana."

"Huh?"

"*Misdirection*, Seaman Broussard. Three: call the Hotel Theresa. Get my usual suite."

"Four?"

"Your boy Patten Leather Mackey. You got a word on him?"

"I ain't got woid on him in ten years, man. Heroin make me noivous…"

"Pin him down any way you can, tell him I need him, quick and quiet. When you're done, meet me on the platform, 'cause we're Broadway bound, baby…"

CHAPTER 9

UPTOWN IN JUNGLE ALLEY

The Pennsylvania Railroad car afforded a much different view than the California Zephyr's: dull and dingy and gun-metal gray rowhouses, warehouses, smokestacks, iron fences and gas storage towers, from D.C. to Newark.

Rocket noted a handful of California Zephyr passengers who'd continued on from Chicago, east, seated up in the first class dining car.

The cover story about the "accident" only worked because Rocket was *invisible* like the Chinese of Harlem. Thus, no one on the Eastern Flyer Limited recognized him as the Negro who'd started out with them on one coast, and was now with them on the other.

He and Bonelip arrived at Pennsylvania Station at 1930 hours. The sun had yet to set; heat and airborne grit still vexed Manhattan.

Even in uniform, the dusky knight and his squat retainer couldn't get a single Red & Yellow cab to take them uptown. The gypsy hacks were more than obliging, however—thanks to the deals they'd struck with the red cap porters to ferry black passengers anywhere.

"Was' the word, admiral! Was' the buzz, Popeye!" crowed the driver of the capacious tan Buick they hailed. "We gotta stop at Times Square to pick up more folk, then we head up Broadway to Amsterdam and stop at—"

"Hold up," interjected Bonelip on his knight's behalf, "Extra ten bones if you roll all the way. And a asswhuppin' if y'all use dem woids 'admiral' or 'Popeye' again, dig?"

"Well shut my mouth! Welcome to New York and climb in!"

The Buick pushed to the Hudson River, hurtled north, then east, then north again around Central Park. Rocket had dreamed of picnicking with Brenda in the park, a carriage ride, a Broadway show. But they never got as far as Baltimore.

When the sun finally dipped behind New Jersey and the street lamps cut on, they were across 110th Street. And there, the island of Manhattan was transformed!

To Rocket's surprise, the cool evening's bustle outpaced the day's sweltering commotion, with tons of folk strolling and strutting up and down Lenox Avenue under the lamplight in their summer finery from Sears & Roebuck or Alexander's or the lucky few from Macy's. Kids marked out hopscotch squares and ringolevio jails in chalk—in total safety and with joyous abandon.

So whether it was ornate brownstone, boxy apartment building or dumbbell tenement—every window was open and bright. Each fire escape and stoop dripped with humanity.

"Smack would mess up alla dis here, boss," pondered Bonelip said, suddenly somber. "Dey hangin' on by dere fingernails as it is. Don Quixote'd be proud a y'all."

"Amen," whispered Rocket. "When's the meet?"

"Wid Mack? After midnight…at the Ubangi Club in Jungle Alley. What 'bout de Smoov Mallard man? Have to keep till Monday, onaccount it's Friday night."

"Nah, he's at the plant on weekends. I'll call him from the hotel."

When the Buick turned onto 125th, the tenements gave way to a light as bright as Fifth Avenue and Times Square combined.

"You gents fixing to go out?" offered the driver. "I can be of service." He reached back to offer his card. "Chauffeur...tour guide. As you can see by the neon way down there by your lodgings, Anita O'Day is the chanteuse tonight at the Apollo. She white, by the way. I believe Lucky Millender is playing up at the Renaissance Ballroom if you gents prefer some dancing, and at—"

"Horse," said Rocket with a banality only a gangster would show. "We want horse. Smack. A score."

The cabbie hit the brakes hard at Seventh, in view of the alabaster Hotel Theresa. "Now look..."

"Do I look like a spade snitchin' for the narko squad?" pressed Rocket. "Where do I score? Some tour guide you are!"

Nervously eyeing Rocket in the rear view mirror, the driver gulped and answered, "I mean...that's maybe east, across Fifth Avenue to Madison. But otherwise, brother, Harlem's dry as a desert."

The light turned green but the Buick was frozen. Horns honked and curses flew as Rocket leaned forward and yanked the driver by his camp shirt collar.

"Dry, huh? What if I don't want what the Italians have got? Don't make me break your neck and steal this fine ride of yours, brothers."

"Alright! Alright! Everybody says the chinks are gonna get something going, make all the dry junkies well. But that's all I know, brother, I swear!"

Settling back in his seat as the Buick pulled in front of the Theresa and its teenage black bellhops, Rocket sighed and revealed, "I'm no junkie, ya hear? And I actually don't want dope. Just jivin' you for info. Say...

what do you do during the day?"

"I-I'm a doorman up at the Hudson View Apartments, Edgecombe Avenue, Sugar Hill. Important folk live up there…like you, right? And I'm a vestryman at Mother Zion AME, praise God!"

"Stay away from the shadows, man." He climbed out, then said, "Pay him, Bonelip. Oh and there's an extra ten-spot if you spill that Rocket Crockett, Naval aviator and derring-doer, is uptown and dancing at the Renaissance, then off to some bourgeois set for cocktails with the braintrust, doctors and lawyers of Edgecombe Avenue."

*****

Around zero-thirty hours a rusted red Nash Airflyte jerked onto Seventh Avenue. Behind the wheel was a Negro with a ragged billy-goat beard, a gold bowling shirt and topped by a moth-chewn flat newsboy cap.

"Come fe git in de car, sah," bid the driver in a Caribbean lilt. "Mackey, 'im waitin'"

"Lawd another damn coconut chaser," groaned Bonelip under his breath.

Rocket pushed his squire inside and away they zoomed, dodging traffic and running red signals.

The driver introduced himself as Donovan Coe, native of Jamaica and "adventurer an' mon o' action come ya-self, Law-tenant Crockett."

"Where's Mackey's creampuff Cadillac ragtop?" quizzed Rocket as the Nash slid down a trash-strewn lane, nipping garbage cans and causing a terrible racket.

"Ahhhh 'im loose it in a likkel disagreement wid de Italians dem ova de Suga Ray Robinson fight." The Nash halted. " 'Ere we are, sah, Jungle Alley."

That dirty piece of West 134th Street was called "Jungle Alley." Most of the establishments were exotic speakeasies in the 20's and 30's like Immerman's and Small's Paradise. Twenty years later, they were gut-bucket joints whose only grace was that star musicians played there after they'd finished sets at classier spots.

The Ubangi Club was the gut-bucket-est of them all, having inaugurated "Coffee Can Thursdays & Fridays." Rocket gaped at the lines of colored folk and a few whites toting empty Yuban and Chock Full' o Nuts cans into the club to be filled with cold Ballantine's or Genessee.

"No wonder dis here alley stinks, boss," observed Bonelip, holding his pug redbone nose.

It was sweltering inside, and thick with cigarette and cigar smoke seasoned with illicit reefer, sweat, spilled beer and cheap perfume. On the sagging stage, a sax player was blowing next to a trumpeter; a drummer, bassist and guitar man wailed behind them. The familiar sights , rhythms and melodies seemed to ease Bonelip's nerves, yet he couldn't abide by these new d; however, couldn't abide these new dances. Part Lindy Hop, part Savoy swing anddrag. Still, for the first time in a year, he watched colored folk celebrating with abandon.

Rocket, however, was scanning the club and marking every face. Just because they were in Jungle Alley, didn't mean they were safe. If the tong could turn someone like Suh on the CIA's payroll, then they could certainly hire a spy to case even this nasty-ass place!

Yet soon Rocket spotted his contacted. Seated in a corner booth Patten Leather Mackey nursed his own bottle of rye. He was a small, thin man with brown skin spotted by age and bad choices. His eyes were hooped and red. He wore a gray homburg on his bald head. Rocket hardly recognized him so frail and beaten down, and Bonelip cringed at the sight of his once robust, twinkled-eyed old pal who'd sponsored champagne Jazz showcases at the Savoy and cut cards with Zora Neale Hurston.

But Patten Leather Mackey could still dress. It was as if the conservative ofays at J.Press had allowed a black man to raid their best shirts, gray flannel creased suits and the glossy black slip-ons which gave him his name. And of course, there was than homburg crown. Once he'd been a prince of Harlem vice. Now he was a has-been—selling reefer, spinning yarns, and drinking in places like the Ubangi Club with the likes of Coe.

Animated after the hugs and hand shakes, Mackey poured rye shots for Rocket, Bonelip and Coe. A waitress, her tight dress squeezing her rear out one end and big bosoms out the other, brought a platter of fried chicken, fried green tomatoes and bite-sized Vienna sausage.

"Dead men are wisest, for they know/How far the roots of the flowers go."

Mackey had been a poetry enthusiast since the good ole days hanging with the likes of Cullen, McKay and Langston Hughes. "And this cat Feng, down Chinatown, he wisest of them all 'cause this cat must've bored a hole to China into the pavement when he took his swan dive offa the IRT track."

"So the Orchids ain't just declaring war on the *goombahs* down on Mulberry Street," surmised Rocket, "they're making their move on the other tongs?"

Patten Leather Mackey nodded. "They goin' for the whole chicken wing, cuz. When running numbers was king up here, not even Madame St. Clair or Dutch Schultz himself had this network for their policy banks. Two dozen chop suey joints and laundries from river to river, accessible west from Jersey, north from the Bronx, south by bridge and tunnel. Brothers, this whole burg becomes one big nasty candy store…"

"For China White," groused Rocket.

"*My soul has grown deep like the rivers*," quoted Mackey. "That's why I swore dealin' off."

Suddenly, Coe offered, "Yah mon, but fe one t'ing. De 'eroin de Coolies dem ya say dey gwine sell—it na 'ere. A duppy-ghost. Nut'ing sa far. Somebody got you chasin' bad info."

"That's not my intel," intoned Rocket, sipping the cheap rye. "Something's coming, or it's already here."

Mackey shrugged. "Dunno, Rocket. The fiends are still hitting the usual pushers. Nothing's changed, everything's on down low, Harlem is pretty much Harlem."

"Yeah," broke in Bonelip, "till Korea ends and someone floods dese here streets wid smack."

Rocket nodded and thought of those Marines at Osan. Should they survive their ordeal in the Punchbowl, they would be coming back to tracks of new yet sterile, identical crackerbox houses and new freeways in treeless subdivisions and dead-end jobs; others would come home to nothing. Both extremes were grim. And whether they were escaping sameness or squalor, heroin would be the ticket out—compliments of Uncle Sam.

"Who can I trust to help me take this down before Harlem blows up?"

"Trust? Ha! Nobody. Not even me. That's why I'm still alive," Mackey said, taking a sausage from the platter. "But there is someone who can help. El Cubano. The old *bolito* king."

Rocket knew "bolito" was the policy or "numbers" racket directed at the Spanish and Caribbean blacks who also flooded Harlem.

"Italians don't mess with him," added Mackey, "and Larry Ma don't know him."

"Larry Ma?"

"Chink hood. Word is he moved uptown from Mott Street to buy up paper on as many of these restaurants and laundries as he can. Loans, gambling debt—hell even kidnapping. Anything to hold over the families owning the place, so they turn the place into a candy store for the dope."

After enduring the last burn of the rye, Rocket said, "Let's go talk to El Cubano."

"He don't come to the Ubangi, Rocket," chuckled Patten Leather Mackey. "He retired and legit, like me. Tonight he's either slumming over in East Harlem with his peoples, or he's up on Sugar Hill with the *niggerati* discussing how Negroes be splitting between the Democrats and this dude Stevenson, or the Republicans and General Ike."

Bonelip chuckled. "Jus' another *Santeria* hoodlum. I got some voodoo for his spic ass."

Mackey recalled Bonelip's old disdain. "Spanish or English, we all colored men, Bonelip. And we all bleed red. He know that, too. That's why I set it up soon's I got your call."

"You still the man, Mackey," grinned Rocket, lifting a glass.

"Meet him at the playground at Madison and 135th at noon tomorrow. Giants are playing the Dodgers up at Coogan's Bluff at one."

"Coogan's Bluff?" frowned Rocket.

"Foreigner!" joked Coe ironically. "Dat de Polo Grounds nickname, Law-tenant. Though me don' knw why dey can't play cricket dere."

"He already got tickets for you," said Mackey. "*A*

common enemy demands an uncommon warrior."

"Is that Langston Hughes?" teased Rocket, "or fellow Howard alum, Gwen Bennett?"

"Nah mon," interposed Coe. "Dat Marcus Garvey Mackey's own verse. De Bard o' Old Broadway!"

"I say we adjourn from this wonderful establishment," prompted Rocket, eyeing the flirtatious women and angry, envious men looking him over. "I want to go where this Feng cat did his high wire act."

"After you," agreed Mackey. "Donovan, tell Miz Queenie to put this mess on my tab, and fetch my silver tip cane."

Little did Rocket know, the pulsing, reeling, smoky and smelly Ubangi Club was the indeed the safest place he'd see in Harlem.

CHAPTER 10

BATTER UP

As Coe and Mackey waited in the idling Nash, Rocket paced around the chalked and blood-stained asphalt. It was the second-to-last thing going through Broken Nose Feng's mind before his ass followed.

You don't put on a show if you don't have an audience. So whoever tossed Feng off the elevated tracks wanted to damn sure make an impression.

"Check it out," called Rocket, pointing across Broadway as the trucks and cars rushed underneath the viaduct. "See what I see, across 126th Street?"

The Big Luck Prime Laundry was dark and gated, but next door, the Big Luck Chop Suey House was lit— and jammed with the children of the night, inviting belly aches to chase their hangovers.

Motioning for the Nash to shadow them, the Black Buccaneer of the Atmosphere and his faithful retainer— resplendent in their summer whites despite the sticky film of the Ubangi Club—strode across the street. The traffic dodged them, of course, rather than the other way around!

When they pushed open the grimy glass door, it was unlike any Western serial Rocket had seen from the colored section of the Cotton King Palace as a kid. For instead of the hushed, turning heads of a silver-screen cowboy saloon, the patrons of the Big Luck kept shoveling pea pods and eggs rolls into their faces as if the sight of two blacks dressed in uniforms was normal.

The people behind the counter, however, had a very different reaction.

A girl Rocket would soon come to know as Mewo had an Auntie Ming, and Auntie Ming, wide-eyed, cried for brother Ri to run to the counter. Ri, manning the steamy woks in the kitchen, came out, cursing, complaining, and tired. He'd have to open the laundry for a few hours.

Soaked with sweat, he froze as if he saw a ghost. Or a guardian angel, clothed in white.

"Two Cokes," ordered Rocket as Bonelip pushed over a sporting gal with door-knocker earrings who'd talked a suburban trick into a bite to eat before the bite to eat.

Ri was transfixed and transfigured. So was Auntie Ming, and her husband.

Yet they knew the face on a yellowed, torn, crumpled flyer that made a miraculous journey from a print shop in Yokohama to an American aircraft carrier, from the pod of a speeding jet to the hands of a hopeful girl to the evil hands of a toad to a chest on a junk, and on a sampan covered in fresh-caught eels to a crate on a tramp freighter covered by mass-produced cocktail umbrellas, to a Chinese herb shop in Honolulu, to a seaplane, to rolling stock in San Pedro to a Chinese restaurant in Trenton to a back-firing vegetable truck crossing the ferry at the Narrows from Staten Island, then across the Brooklyn Bridge. And uptown…

Ri fainted on the spot.

But commotion in the restaurant was soon overshadowed by a ruckus on the street.

A fat maroon '49 Cadillac convertible stuffed with sun-tanned and silk-clad white men had cut across the ragged Nash; several of the group clambered out, Louisville Sluggers in hand, and began beating the already beaten car. Two more were holding Mackey and Coe at bay with a shotgun and a .38.

"Where da po-lice at?" shouted Bonelip.

"Seventy-Seventh Precinct," Auntie Ming's husband said from the greasy tile floor, trying to revive Ri. "They no look when *bakgwei* pay off."

Without a word, Rocket and Bonelip shoved through the confused patrons to the sidewalk. Bonelip hid in the dark while Rocket stepped in the glow of the neon "Chop Suey" sign, hands high, hands empty.

The traffic on Broadway continued as if it was a normal late-night occurrence.

"Whoze the *mouli* in the Navy whites?" called the *capo* of the bat-wielding hoods to underlings.

"Anchors away!" signaled Rocket.

From under his white sailor blouse Bonelip produced the .45 and tossed it like a short stop to a second basemen. In a fluid motion honed by much practice on scarier men than these, Rocket caught it, yanked the slide, spun and aimed.

Bam-Bam-Bam-Bam! Four shots, four hits, none lethal unless someone eschewed a trip to the hospital! The armed men fell first; two of batters limped away. The rest jumped into the car but were subdued by Coe before the driver could floor it.

"I thrash ya, ya bumbaclots you!" shouted the Jamaican as he walloped the Mob soldiers.

Mackey swung his steel-tipped cane, too, like in the old days. Bonelip chased the stragglers, who rallied only to collect their wounded and escape up the IRT platform on the viaduct.

Before the first green bulbous Plymouth NYPD radio

cars showed, Rocket turned toward the plate glass of the Big Luck. Auntie Ming and her husband had helped Ri to his feet.

A slop cook Rocket would hardly notice any other time was bawling like a child, yet laughing as he stumbled out to the sidewalk to tug on Rocket's arm. "You...you come help! Thank you...thank you!"

Knowing he had to stash the .45 before the cops arrived, Rocket backed off.

"Why is Larry Ma threatening you? He had Feng murdered, didn't he?"

Still, all Ri could do was blubber in adulation. Yet in this man's weird exuberance Rocket sensed something. Something plugging a hole Mae's story, and filled Abensour's manipulative half-truths.

"*You know me?*" pressed Rocket.

Before Ri could answer, Coe wheeled the commandeered Caddie in a screeching three-point turn on Broadway, and scooped up Mackey and Bonelip.

"Come on, man!" hollered Bonelip to Rocket. With sirens bearing down, Rocket cursed and jumped into the car. But he never broke his gaze at the old man as the whitewalled monster thundered toward St. Nicholas.

"Hot dog!" rejoiced Mackey from capacious rear seat. "*And there in the pallor of moon-veiled light/The loveliest things were seen.*"

"What's the buzz?" pressed Bonelip, heart racing, taking the Colt from a distant-minded Rocket.

"Ha!" gushed Coe. "Dis 'im car, mon!"

Apparently this was the creampuff Caddie that Mackey'd lost in the Sugar Ray Robinson wager.

"Fate woiks in mad ways, eh boss?" mused Bonelip.

Rocket nodded, pensive despite the violence.

"Don't forget DeWitt at Smoov Mallard," reminded

Bonelip. "You runnin' low. Check yo' hair. "

*****

The crowd of cherubic and delinquent teens had grown to perhaps a hundred; even the little girls had abandoned their jump ropes and jacks to see the next pitch.

At the "plate" was a skinny black man in pleated trousers and a red short sleeved knit shirt. He took some practice cuts with the "bat"—a broomstick wrapped with electrician tape at the grip. His toothy grin signaled his readiness as he stepped up.

The pitcher was a coffee-skinned man with nappy, snow white hair and amber eyes. He looked to be the grandfather of every kid out there.

"Hokey, batta," called the pitcher, winding up, "Jou betta be in chape, 'cause ee' comin' *a fuego*!"

The black rubber ball flew and bounced as planned, but Willie Mays eyed it perfectly and smacked it high over the "left field fence"—a laundry line fluttering with shirts and sheets.

Willie guffawed; El Cubano, though he threw a homer, bid the crowd to cheer. After a mock run of the bases, Willie came in for hugs and photographs with the kids.

"Lotta fun, man, lotta fun," giggled the young rookie, "but now I gotta head to the Bluff."

But El Cubano wasn't going to let him get away that easily. "Before jou go I wan' jou to me' mi bery goo' fren' …de hero 'Rocke-ay' Crocke-ay. Yet airplane ace!"

Rocket, back in his service dress khakis, shook Mays' hand. "An honor."

"*Say-hey*," replied Mays. "You're the fella Mr.

Pompez says needs a mess of autographs for the troops, eh? I'll get 'em to you right after the game. Mine, Monte's…even Mr. Durocher's!"

Mays waved and jumped in a cab hailed by one of El Cubano's goons.

Public relations ploy ceased, Alejandro Pompez—a.k.a El Cubano—wiped off his smile and took Rocket for a serious stroll up Madison Avenue.

"I hear jou had a lil' trouble las' night. Had I known…"

"Better you didn't."

"Whas jou doin' here, *compay*? This not jour style. Mackey, he say jou on some crusade?"

Rocket laughed, shook his head.

El Cubano stopped, gestured with three fingers as he slouched toward Rocket.

"Wi'out a angle, a man is nothin' but a chump. A chump wi' ballz, *si*. But a chump none-de-less."

"My angle is my business, Mr. Pompez. Your angle is survival, if this war between the Chinese and the Italians materializes. And, I can kick you a lil' bita cash."

"Cash is goo', *compay*. Cash is always goo…"

"But let's be frank. Nothing's gonna restore the power you once had. You're a dinosaur. So rather than just die out, how about taking one last big bite?"

Pompez halted at Rocket's impertinence, as did the two brown-skinned, sable-haired henchmen flanking them. He glowered at Rocket for a second, then broke into laughter.

"*Si, madre*…ballz! Was jou need from me, hero?"

"Your muscle, when I make the call. Plus you're to guard my friends up here, and any friends I make." Rocket paused, surveying the block, then said, "And stay outta the way of the Office of Naval Intelligence, other g-men who might come looking for me. They can get scary."

"Spies and cops, huh?" chuckled El Cubano. "*Oigame compay*, J. Ed-har Hoover try to deport me when I buy de Dyckman Oval up Washington Height...I own two Negro League team there, main. But I still here. De goo-er-men don't scare me. Les' hit de ballpark."

The Giants won, 6-3, though the Harlem crowd upset the Giants' white fans by rooting for the Dodger players they liked. Despite the compassion, Don Newcombe was chased out in the fourth inning. Campenella and Jackie went hitless. Branca was awful in relief and Gil Hodges' two doubles were the only bright spot for Brooklyn. Bobby Thompson homered twice—portents of something bad for the Dodgers come Autumn, Rocket predicted.

As the crowd filed out of the Polo Grounds, El Cubano pointed to Leo Durocher ambling from the dugout to the massive scoreboard in right field.

"*Mira aqui*," laughed Pompez in a sinister tone, "He stealing de signs from de catchers, main. No' luck, no' fate, no' even Santeria *ogun*." He made a weird genuflection at the word "ogun," to be safe. "Life is a angle. A edge. Jou ready?"

"I'm ready," nodded Rocket. "Let's bring some pain."

El Cubano shook Rocket's hand. "Larry Ma, like de Dodgers, gon' to get a big surprise, eh? Don' forget jou autographs in de clu'house. And there a surprise for jou in there. A present."

"Mr. Pompez, you shouldn't have."

Though El Cubano didn't know whether Rocket was for real or busting his chops, he still smiled. "Crusaders, they need a holy weapon, eh? 'Cause eve' though they chumps...*mira*...they still got ballz. Enjoy."

Rocket got a number of autographed photos at the 156th Street entrance, near the clubhouse. And a bat, compliments of Pompez. He could go downtown and get a bat at Gimbels. But this was the game bat, still stained with a little pine tar—and autographed and dated that day by Willie Mays and Jackie Robinson.

CHAPTER 11

FOR HAIR THAT LAYS DOWN AND SHINES

The Wing Fat Sino-American Trading Company on Mott Street was the Orchid Tong's legit front in Chinatown. Even the bunko cops and the FBI knew that.

What they didn't know, and what El Cubano revealed to Rocket, was that the company now leased an old coaling pier and dilapidated coal bunker on the Hudson, just below the cliffs where 135th Street ended. The signatory on the lease was one Xi Pin "Lawrence" Ma, humble import-export insurance broker .

Pompez even had a photograph. The pier itself looked like dead black fingers coming out of the water; the dank building was home to pigeons and rats. The place had been abandoned since many homes and tenements modernized from coal delivery after the last war.

And so, while Rocket and Patten Leather Mackey headed downtown in a newly washed and waxed '49 Cadillac convertible, Bonelip and Coe staked out the pier from a car Coe boosted from one of the local numbers thugs.

Though delayed by a jack-booted motorcycle cop's nuisance stop, the Caddie finally rumbled by the three story brick and stone building festooned with streamers and paper lanterns.

Wing Fat sold oriental decorations and accoutrements popular with the burgeoning suburb dweller class, especially for their warm weather cookouts and cocktail hours. Thus Mott Street was clogged with Oriental and Occidental shoppers alike.

Wing Fat also stocked wholesale kitchen and laundry supplies,; the latter including soaps, refurbished clothing press machinery, dry cleaning chemicals, and powdered starch. *Anything you need as a front to cook, mix and cut dope*, mulled Rocket inwardly.

"That old man in the chop suey joint," prompted Mackey, "Broussard says you all shared a moment?"

"Dunno," said Rocket, lifting his Ray Bans to survey the block with keen eyes, "but circling back there is part of closing the links to this chain."

"A chain you don't know what's at the damn center of. Could be around your own neck."

Mackey adjusted his diamond tie pin when a pair of comely Chinese girls in pink floral dresses and shaded by paper parasols strolled by the car, ogling Rocket. Mackey was happy for the indirect attention.

"And by the way, Rocket, what you got wrapped up in the trunk of my car? If it's a rifle and that ofay cop woulda found it, it's back to Sing Sing for me."

"A present," boasted Rocket, sunglasses back on and attention toward the building. "No goons outside, nothing that would indicate they were at war with the other tongs…"

"This is Chinatown, jack. Nothing here is what it seems."

The Cadillac rolled down Mott to Bayard Street then pulled up, slowly, to an alley off Pell Street. Rocket jumped out while Mackey kept the V-8 running.

Knowing there were likely eyes on him, Rocket loped up to a place where the alley widened to a truck-turning bay. There he found the loading dock of the Wing Fat.

The alley smelled like week-old cabbage and motor oil; he could hear men and women yammering and arguing in Mandarin, Catonese and pigin English.

Beneath the loading dock, Rocket spied something stuck to his shoe. It clumped like un-sifted flour but with a grainer texture and nutty smell. Powdered starch. There was more—in clumps, as if someone had muffed an entire sack—and there were many footprints in it other than his own. It was leading out, not into, the now-padlocked metal door of the building.

Something was on the move. And Rocket knew where.

Before Rocket could reach the idling car, three Chinese men materialized into the shafts of sunlight cutting in from above. All three were young punks with greased hair, torn up white tee shirts, dungarees, and boots. Two dangled long chains with barbed hooks on the end. The third cut the air with a meat cleaver.

Instantly Rocket sensed his advantage. It was the narrow neck of that stinking alley. The clowns with the chains could only come at him one at a time or risk fouling a comrade. And Mackey, though old and infirm, was close.

"Fellas, fellas," mugged Rocket, tossing off his combination cap and Ray Bans. "Don't use duck fat in your hair. Use the duck. Smoov Mallard works. I don't even have to use a stocking cap, no lie."

One of the young hoodlums hurled his chain. Rocket ducked the hook but caught a few links. With a mighty tug and shout, he yanked the kid forward and off balance, right into the path of his onrushing, screaming, cleaver-swinging pal. With a thud, they slammed together and broke apart onto the pavement.

Rocket kicked the cleave-wielder's head down onto

a manhole cover. The kid got a roundhouse kick to the chest as he attempted to rise. Sure enough, the third punk could only swing the chain above his head, menacingly, yet powerless to help.

It was a standoff as the two circled each other in the narrow passage, Rocket eyeing the arcs of that hook, until the blare of the Cadillac's yacht-like horn signaled the end of the fight for thug number three. As he turned away from Rocket he was greeted by the chrome steel grill of the biggest car he'd ever seen.

With a thump, he was down.

"Come on!" Mackey hollered as Rocket retrieved his cap, then checked the wounded attackers for tattoos. No orchids or orchid characters. Quickly, he hopped in and Mackey one-hand-wheeled that gargantuan piece of Detroit machinery in reverse…fast, and without losing a hair's breadth of paint.

"Orchids?" puffed Mackey, more out of breath than Rocket as they motored toward the Bowery.

"Nah," mulled Rocket, straightening his tie. "I was just a random trespasser and that was the bush league rear-guard. The real bad men have bugged out—uptown."

"Those items you asked me to get when you left the ballpark…got 'em in the back here. The Army-Navy store says they only have a range of a mile. Would felt better getting s'more guns."

Rocket reached behind the seat and pulled up a World War Two-vintage walkie talkie. Bonelip had the other working unit. This one had a busted mini-vacuum tube. With the radio parts stores on the West Side and them on the East, the only play was to hit a hardware store there on Delancey. But time was wasting…

Rocket purchased the part and hit a phone booth at the luncheonette next door. He called the Hotel Theresa for messages.

The last normal message was from Mr. DeWitt, president of Smoove Mallard. He was calling about a black tie party given by Mr. W.E.B. DuBois for a neighbor, an NAACP lawyer named Marshall who'd scored a big court win against Jim Crow crackers in Oklahoma.

But the most recent message was hardly normal. The Hotel Theresa switchboard operator indeed recounted that it was Mr. DeWitt again, but he sounded frantic and railed about a "Chinaman" whom DeWitt had already thrown out of his office a few days earlier when he began "blabbering" about a daughter. The man had come back, and was "jabbering" again—this time about Rocket coming all the way from *Shanghai*, China of all places, to help him. "I know this sounds pretty wacky, Lieutenant," the young woman concluded. "Lieutenant Crocket?"

Rocket let the phone slip from his hand. He turned, slowly, to Mackey in the Cadillac. "We gotta bounce!"

*****

Bonelip had changed into his blue service dungarees and shirt for the mission. He and Coe parked off Riverside and ambled to the cliffs to get a better view of the coal pier with a set of binoculars.

" 'ey, bwoy," called Coe, fiddling with the walkie talkie. " 'ow dis speak? It look like a shoebox wid a knittin' needle stuck on de top!"

"Ain't no toy, man," scolded Bonelip, scanning the river. "Hope Rocket got de other one woikin'. You jus' keep it on for a spell den cut it off den back on, ya hear?"

All Coe got was static. But Bonelip saw something strange in the binoculars. A boat, about the size of a Navy launch, cut through the heat shimmer on the Hudson. The deck above the cabin portholes was jammed with men.

Two black cars pulled up on the street fronting the shore. Out jumped a group of men the in dark pajama-like outfits Bonelip recalled only Chinese men wore. But one character was clothed in a white summer suit, white fedora, and white and brown spectator shoes.

"Dang," muttered Bonelip, "enough orientals down dere ta build a Great Wall to da Bronx." He turned to Coe. "Press dat switch and call for Rocket."

No reply.

"*Alors*...it's jus' you and me. Let's go..."

They scrambled to the car and floored it down to the 135th Street cut. Ditching the car, they ran to the warehouses adjacent to the property.

*****

"Cops on us!" warned Mackey as the Caddie sped up the East River Drive.

A radio car and a motorcycle had been tailing the Cadillac since it departed the Bowery. Again, not unusual for them to harass colored men in a colorful car. But there was no time to deal with that mess.

It turned into a full-scale siren-wailing chase once they crossed under the Queensboro Bridge.

Peeling off his cap to keep it from blowing away, Rocket called to Mackey, "I'm sorry I got you into this... all over a pipedream, sorta, eh?"

That homburg remained glued on Mackey's brown, wrinkled dome, despite the windwash. "You kiddin', brother?" The V-8 was just warming up as the Caddie sling-shotted around Gracie Mansion. "*Yet I do marvel at this curious thing/To make a poet black and bid him sing*! I ain't had this much fun in years, jack!"

The flatfoots were no match for this machine. They started to fade when the Harlem River split off from the East River and the stubby drawbridges to the Bronx came into view.

More cars were likely on the way, but Patten Leather Mackey knew all of the run n' ditch routes as he careened onto 135th, zooming west to Broadway.

Spinning into an alley, the Caddie stopped and its occupants sank below the dashboard.

"Take the walkie talkie," ordered Rocket, "Contact Bonelip. I'm gonna shoe-leather it up to 143rd. You need me, call me at Hamilton 7-0999. Got it?"

Mackey drove off as if he was once again a proper gangster.

Rocket moved up the block, tipping his hat to strolling passers. He found the long, red brick building planted between the rows of apartments, painted with huge yellow letters: "SMOOV MALLARD HAIR PRODUCTS & BARBER SUPPLIES." There was the duck logo, with shiny green on his nape.

And sure enough, plastered across the ground floor service door and windows facing the subway stop were posters of Lt. Rufus "Rocket" Crockett, USN—his hair laid down and shining.

A lady in a broad church hat who was pushing a baby pram stopped when she recognized him.

"Oh my! That's *you*?"

Rocket touched his finger to his lips and winked. He knew that DeWitt kept a key to that door in a compartment in the jamb. The lady decided to swoon rather than move, and a growing gaggle, all featuring their best dresses and Sunday crowns, headed toward him.

"Maranantha! Louise! Alma! Trixie! Ladies! This

dashing hero has come to Harlem and we have him all to ourselves!"

After asking him to which church he belonged and whether he could come to their club meeting that night and what his favorite meal was, Rocket finally brokered a deal upon seeing a lady toting an Eastman camera. One picture, then they had to let him tend his business.

A bystander herded the group together, with Rocket—now holding the baby boy—at the center. Two snaps and it was over, with the bystander demanding a dollar.

"Ain't no one in there today, sir," the young man said, pocketing his payment, "but I did see some folk coming in the office entrance before church. "Look like the custodian let 'em in with Mr. DeWitt."

"Was the visitor an old Chinese man?"

"No sir."

"Wait, what?"

"It was a Chinese *lady*, some other Chinese man she was holding onto, and a younger cat, sorta rough looking…like he just left a chink rent party. She ain't look to happy to be with that younger fella."

Rocket slid the fellow another dollar, found the key and slipped in.

The cavernous storage room was piled to the iron beams with cardboard boxes of pomade ready to be shipped. Pallets were loaded with bottles and tins of hair tonic, aftershave, ingrown hair balm and shaving cream—all waiting to be packed by workers Monday morning.

Beneath Rocket's feet was the heart of the plant: cooking and rendering vats, distilling and titrating tubes, fragrance bins. The pumps and conveyors weren't idle; as the weekend shift was due in a few hours the machinery hummed, awaiting the humans to turn it full-bore. And down there, tubs of dangerous chemicals bubbled and roiled. The place's subterranean innards were more confusing and disorienting than belowdecks on *Bonhomme Richard.*

It was stifling inside the plant, though the slit windows were tilted open. But it was what Rocket found in DeWitt's office that chilled him to the bone.

Blood on the carpet. Papers scattered. DeWitt's pipes and tobacco decanter broken and busted. And a shoe. Moreso, a slipper. The kind a Chinese woman would wear.

The phone rang and Rocket hesitated, then answered, in a whisper, after closing the glass door. "Hullo?"

Mackey was panting as he recited: *"Them flowers came from that poor boy's friends—They'll want flowers, too, when they meet their ends."*

"Man, I got a situation here," whispered Rocket, "so speak in prose, damn it."

"We gotta situation here too, brother. No Broussard, no Coe. I turnt on that radio and all I got was some dudes jibber-jabbering in Chinese. Something's dead wrong."

Rocket swallowed hard. "Get up here, fast. Do *not* call. Park on 143rd."

Rocket hung up when he saw a figure silhouetted in the tinted and faceted glass panel. He hit the deck, waited.

The office door creaked open. From behind DeWitt's chair, Rocket could see a pair of lace-ups, no socks, moving across the floor. A voice in Chinese was out in the hall asking if the room was clear.

The man who'd come inside the office responded in Chinese, which Rocket made out to be: *"Go check the dogs in the basement."*

Rocket could see he was brandishing an old German

Luger 9mm. "*I will call Ma.*," the man said, tucking the pistol in his waistband.

Rocket circled away, crablike, as the man searched DeWitt's desk for the phone. Strangely, it rang again. Yet as the man reached for the receiver, he noticed a tautness to the line. He bent over to check it. It was the last move he would ever make.

Rocked popped up from the floor, ripped the phone line from the wall and snared the man's neck. He pulled till a wheeze and a purple tongue signaled one less Orchid flunky.

Pocketing the Luger, Rocket made his way to basement, gingerly creeping down a circular steel staircase.

It didn't take long to find three people hog-tied, gagged, and laying side by side under a pipe to the scent vats. DeWitt had a bloody bandage on his head but was alert enough to widen his eyes, mumble under the gag and squirm. Beside him, a Chinese woman and man were also squirming.

Two of the folks from the chop suey joint…

With his pen knife, Rocket cut DeWitt loose first, but not before he held his fingers to his lips and gestured. The other hoodlum was around, somewhere. He gave the knife to DeWitt, still woozy, then snuck toward the distilling tubes and towers, Luger drawn.

Suddenly Rocket heard something whizz by his ear, then a plink of metal hitting metal, then another whizz. This time, he felt a sharp pain in his shoulder. Disoriented, he ducked under a short catwalk, reached and pulled a red-tasseled brass dart from his deltoid.

"You son of a bitch," growled Rocket as he heard footsteps on the catwalk. He knew he'd only have a minute or so before whatever the Orchids dip their *biao* in took effect.

Rocket aimed for a water pipe on the wall and fired. The water gushed as Rocket rolled away, firing at a distilling tower which leaked alcohol and something deadly and anise-scented. The distraction allowed him time to scale the catwalk as the stalker moved to its opposite end.

"Surprise!" taunted Rocket.

But before he could fire, this nimble henchman did an acrobat's flip and dove off the edge while sending another dart sailing past Rocket's face. Worse, the Luger jammed despite Rocket mashing the ancient top-toggle action. He dropped the gun, eyes blurry.

"Help!" Rocket heard DeWitt's scream. A female's shriek echoed after it.

Bounding off the catwalk as the poison slowly numbed his limbs, Rocket returned to find the stalker holding a square-bladed knife to Auntie Ming's fleshy throat. The thug barked for Rocket to back off.

Injured but determined, DeWitt grabbed the man's ankle sending him stumbling.

The gamble allowed Auntie Ming to slough her captor's arm and scamper away—just as Rocket pounced.

Wrestling knives from murderous thugs had become second nature for Rocket. But never before had the room been spinning. A Sugar Ray Robinson upper cut finally loosed the knife and a few of the attacker's teeth. The henchman retreated to the catwalk with Rocket in groggy pursuit. Out of darts, the man lunged for the Luger, unaware that it was virtually useless.

Thanks to DeWitt's spendthrift attitude on maintenance, the catwalk shuddered as bolts popped and framing gave way. It wasn't built for running and combat.

One side dropped first, and unfortunately for the smirking Tong member, it was his. He slid off into a vat of rendering solution, judging by the smell of it and the attacker's screams of agony.

Stumbling backward, Rocket showed Auntie Ming and DeWitt the dart wound. Ming's husband suddenly appeared, carrying a handful of green sprigs. He held up a hankerchief that reeked of the anise-smelling chemical now spilling on the floor, then motioned for Rocket to remove his shirt.

He poured the chemical on the wound and Rocket howled. Then he gestured for Rocket to chew the green herbs.

"I'll be," sputtered DeWitt. "That's thyme leaves and stems we use for the hair tonic…"

Auntie Ming's husband nodded and smiled. "It good medicine."

DeWitt's heroics finally did him in. He was now unconscious on the floor. Rocket grabbed the passed-out executive's fountain pen. Hurriedly, he grabbed a clipboard, scribbled something on a factory form. He tore off the paper and stuffed it into his trouser pocket.

Auntie Ming burst from the building first, followed by her husband and Rocket carrying DeWitt between them.

From the luncheonette across 143rd came the church ladies Rocket had entertained not minutes before.

"Young man, what happened?" gasped one. Even the curly-haired baby sat up in the pram to point. "You're hurt!"

"Ma'am I been hurt all day. Call the police and Harlem Hospital—there's been a robbery and assault. Tell them it was men from Chinatown and make sure you give my name, got it?"

The women nodded in unison.

The Cadillac rolled up. Before jumping in, Rocket handed the torn paper to another lady.

"Call that number. Tell the person this exact message: it's on, at the river. They'll know."

"B-But…"

The Caddie rumbled away as one women, hands on her hip, shot, "Well don't just stand there Maranantha—get to dialing, girl!"

"Your hair's still laying down, man," complimented Mackey.

"And shining…" said Rocket sternly.

Chapter 12

Showdown on the River

There was now just one guard posted outside of the coal building so as not to rouse the curiosity of both cops and West Harlem denizens. Still, he was dressed in *changshan* and wide-leg coolie pants, so anyone could have asked why he was so far north of Canal Street. Of course that person would be dead after asking.

And still no word from Bonelip or Coe.

Under the rumble of traffic from the Henry Hudson Parkway overhead, Rocket tossed his torn and bloody khaki service shirt into the trunk of the Cadillac and retrieved a slender, three-foot-long item sheathed in orange and black tissue paper.

"Halloween?" quipped Mackey, slipping on black leather gloves.

"Unh-unh. New York Giants." He unwrapped the autographed baseball bat, made some cuts in the air. "Though a little Dodger blue's on here."

"That ain't gonna do you no good," laughed Mackey, removing a suitcase from the Cadillac. He popped it open and lifted out a Thompson submachine gun from the good ole days. He clipped in the drum magazine. "Sure you don't wanna trade, youngbuck?"

With a sly grin, Rocket answered, "Nah I'm good. Try them one last time."

Mackey called on the walkie talkie, and this time, he

got an answer.

"Mi sorry, bushaman Mackey, *ova*…" Coe's voice crackled, low and furtive.

"That you, Donovan? What the hell, man?"

"Shush na Mackey. Mi one an' Broussard ambushed by de coolies dem. Broussard, 'im one get snatched. Dey beat de man but me nah t'ink 'im talk. Mi one at the dockside door, to de leff of de pier. 'urry mon…*ova*."

Rocket exchanged quizzical looks with Mackey. Their underlings weren't amateurs when it came to tactics and keeping their wits—so what could've gone wrong?

Moreover, both men sensed something bizarre in Coe's tone and words. He'd once cracked that he'd never seen a walkie talkie except in Terry and The Pirates in the funny papers. Yet now he's adept, even saying "over?"

"Take my watch and ring," said Rocket, his eyes stapled to the river, unblinking.

Mackey, older and out of breath and still sporting his homburg, took up a position behind the thick steel of the Cadillac. Rocket, shirtless and barefoot so not to make any sound, scrambled—bat in hand—to the wall opposite the lone patrolling guard.

Into the murky water of the Hudson he slipped, bobbing with the bat as he made his way along the broken pier, outflanking the guard and anyone else looking.

Sure hope this autograph ink's waterproof…

Rocket pinpointed the door where Coe claimed to be stationed. Instead, he found another tong hoodlum on patrol, smoking a cigarette. Finding his footing on the ropes wrapped around a piling, Rocket climbed out of the water…

Swoosh!—a wet home run to the noggin.

Rocket grabbed the limp body and lowered it into

the drink.

From inside the ramshackle structure, he heard Coe's distinctive accent. There wasn't a hint of stress in it.

The rickety, ruined door opened easily. There was Coe, alright—pacing, running his mouth.

Rocket slid in and Marine-crawled among the debris and coal dust, the bat out in front. Thankfully, the rookie's and icon's signatures were still there!

"Ya bumbaclot cotton-picka betta talk," Coe shouted at some unseen victim. "Dese coolies gotta way o' cut-tin' on a mon what make 'im talk. So, is Crockett 'im bringin' de Navy 'ere? 'ow much 'im know about shipment o' China White to replace what 'im one burn up?"

Against the backdrop of a rusted giant coal chute and rustier iron reticulated gate, Bonelip sat, tied to a chair, blood clotted in his wide nostrils.

Now on Coe's blindside, Rocket rose, slowly, like a hooded cobra.

"Hey, Benedict Arnold," hissed the derring-doer, back in the thick of it.

Rocket jammed the bat into Coe's ribs, then shot the handle across Coe's nose. The Jamaican dropped and Rocket jumped onto him, shoving the bat crosswise under Coe's chin.

"*Hush*…is the China White on the boat moored out there, or is it in here?"

"Y-You gwine be dead anyway," spit Coe. "Mi one jus' join de winnin' team."

Semi-conscious, Bonelip muttered, "*Rock*-et," then motioned with his head.

The rusty coal chute swung away, moved by the same gears that now raised the metal gate. A flock of pigeons, along with Rocket, was flushed by the screeching metal parts and movement.

There, standing in the room an army of thugs—some armed with guns, some with exotic swords—was a smirking Larry Ma.

Rocket, wet and smeared black with coal grime, rose to his bare, dirty feet. He pointed with the bat.

"Too bad you all didn't take to baseball like the Japanese did." For good measure, he stomped the prone Coe in his chest. The Chinese laughed.

"We play game," spit Larry Ma, hands in his pockets. "Call *lingchi*. You find out what mean soon, hotshot."

"Where's the dope?

Another voice, in perfect English and laced with a British accent, chirped from a deep pocket of the wrecked building.

"Patience, Lieutenant. First we have loose ends to snip."

Flanked by two cronies, a short, well-groomed Chinese man in a seersucker suit, white buck shoes and a gold and purple bow tie, appeared in the light sunlight pouring through the holes in the ceiling. Tortoise shell spectacles covered his small eyes. He smiled to show a mouth full of silver.

"My name is White Paper Fan, your humble servant. So rare I get to America. And so rare we have the bloody good sport of…how do you say…killing many birds with one stone?"

White Paper Fan snapped orders to Larry Ma in Chinese, and as he did, Bonelip said to Rocket, "I'm sorry, boss. "

"You didn't do anything wrong," smiled Rocket as Ma's henchmen approached. But quickly he whispered, "the walkie?"

Bonelip moved his eyes to a spindly table near his

chair then muttered, "Able…Oboe Oboe…"

Affirmative…on and operational. Hopefully Coe didn't lock the switch.

Rocket would find out now, as a bloody Coe lifted himself off up to shove Rocket forward toward Ma's footsoldiers. One flunky took the bat, the other held a sword to the small of Rocket's back and pointed him to White Paper Fan.

Ma's other stooges brought in Uncle Ri. His hands were bound, his head was down.

"Lieutenant," began White Paper Fan, "we have here a convergence of *chi* flow. A hero in need of heroic purpose, a most unfortunate slight on someone who should never be slighted, a business opportunity…and, a damsel in distress. To wit…"

From behind Ri came a rough looking female hoodlum, towing a pretty young Chinese woman with short, feathered and bobbed black hair. She was clothed in a narrow, hip-hugging skirt that ended at her knees and a silk sleeveless blouse—as if someone had tried to tart her up for their amusement.

Trembling, she muttered, in English, "M-My name is Julie Wang…"

"Shut mouth Xui-Ling!" bleated Larry Ma.

After a glance from White Paper Fan, Ma was the one who shut up.

"Mr. Rocket…" whimpered Julie.

Smiling to calm her, Rocket said, "Call me Rufus, honey."

"Oh no…you 'Rocket.' My Auntie Ming, she see newspaper from San Francisco—you, at fire. We send news back home. Then," she cut her eyes at Larry Ma, "they come, for me, because they want use my father. My father escape Communists just to be slave again…

because I weak. Then God bring a message from sky. You come to Shanghai. Cousin Mewo rejoices, sends message here. We know…hair place is where you would come."

"See?" grinned White Paper Fan. "Convergence. *Quod erat demonstrandum.*"

Rocket whispered to tremulously to Julie, and her unseen cousin, so far away, "I'm sorry… I let you down."

Julie's tears claimed her. "But you came. That mean fate bring you."

"This like soap opera on radio!" raved Larry Ma. "We kill now, please?"

"Loathe as I am, Lieutenant, to agree with this sot, yes. But you are coming with me."

The echoed crackle of static came from Bonelip's direction. Bewildered, some of the captors looked around for the source.

Rocket looked to Ri, then to Julie. He puffed out his chest and shouted, "So I'm leaving…but the rest of you, by the truck entrance, and the left, away from the pier, are staying?"

Suddenly, there was another crackle of static from the dumped walkie talkie, and the words, *"Bateador aqui!"*

Coe winced, as he understood what was happening. *"De 'ell fyah fi you*, Rocket Crockett!"

Thank-you, church ladies! A second later a red-chassis Studebaker truck exploded through the rotted bay doors.

Simultaneously, Mackey's Caddie tore through the tar-paper wall to Rocket's left as if it were built out of butter. The old Jazz gangster jumped up from the driver's seat and loosed an old-school barrage from his ancient Tommy gun.

Springing from the truck came El Cubano's goons.

One armed with a shotgun laid down a spray to mow the row for his comrades who wielding crowbars, chains and axe handles. All of them were under orders to cancel anyone Chinese.

Since that included Ri and Julie, Rocket charged and pushed them to the floor, out of harm's way.

Two of Ma's men pounced, but Rocket dispatched one with a *jujitsu* flip and an elbow to the face; a kick to the adam's apple took care of the other.

Rocket directed Pompez's boys to cut Bonelip free as he scooped up his bat. "Then take these folks and him outta here!"

Swinging like Josh Gibson, Rocket cut through the Orchid, and was the only warrior disregarding the flying lead as the battle ebbed and surged between gangs.

Coe tried to crawl through a hole in the dilapidated wall leading out to the pier, but Rocket saw Mackey pen him in with a burst of Thompson fire, then another, as if Coe was a puppy scampering back and forth.

"Mi beg ya, Mack! Mi do ya slave service fe'eva!"

Mackey took aim and froze the Jamaican on his knees long enough for Bonelip to bust the chair he'd been bound to over Coe's head.

Quickly Rocket spotted White Paper Fan and one of his surviving retainers trying to beat feet toward the pier and the bobbing boat. Police sirens on land and water, closing fast, paused the bashing and shooting.

"I'm goin' for the cheese!" Rocket yelled to Bonelip.

White Paper Fan scampered to the river's edge, only to see two police boats closing in. A voice on a loudspeajer demanded his surrender or death.

Smiling, Rocket turned to see El Cubano's men and Mackey pull away in their vehicles, with Bonelip, Ri and Julie huddled in the back of the Studebaker truck.

On shore, the caravan of cop cars included two gray sedans stenciled with "US Navy." Abensour got the message. Better late than never. They'd find a new shipment of dope here somewhere.

Triumphant, Rocket stood tall with his bat…until a face in the shadows caught his attention. A woman's face. Beautiful. Oriental. With stygian lips. The lips blew a kiss.

It was as if tiny shards of glass tore through Rocket's nostrils, trachea, eyes and tongue.

Then all sound ceased, and everything went as black as those lips…

CHAPTER 13

SHANGHAIED

Rocket thought he was dead. A stray bullet? A sword cut from an Orchid Tong thug? He was sad. He'd never see Brenda again. At least he'd find Sammy...

He remembered the face: the black lips. And again, the terror washed over him. No, this wasn't death. It was worse.

He couldn't move, but he could blink. No matter, for he was engulfed in darkness. He couldn't scream, yet his mouth was almost glued shut from dehydration. Against his back and legs, he could feel the confines of what was an oblong box. Ozone filled his nostrils. His ears popped from pressure; there was the familiar hum of plane props. A lot of them.

Rocket screamed, inwardly, until that thing that kept him alive and alert in so many battles welled up, calmed him...

...*think, you mutha, think*...

Yes, the props! He listened to their timing and strokes for hours. And despite a few slight pitches and yaws, there was smooth air. He sensed the altitude, but there was no loss of pressure or oxygen...

... a Stratocruiser? No ... a Lockheed Constellation ... I'm over mountain updrafts ...

Indeed, Rocket had been paralyzed, in a coma, through the first legs of his journey, from Idlewild to

Madrid, Madrid to Paris. This was the Paris to Saigon run, after a refueling stop.

Such was the long journey of the young widow of Dewei Zhou Ping, Chinatown restaurateur and banker, taking her husband's remains to rest among his ancestors. The Pacific route was boring, she told the customs and TWA officials at Idlewild. She'd always wanted to see the old Silk Road route from the air. They stamped her passport and pressed a seal on the death certificate copy.

She was an exotically attractive woman, though she kept to herself, snug in her fur stole. She used a lacquered cigarette holder and always wore her gloves, as this was a luxury flight.

Her companion was a pigtailed servant, whose appearance, inapt to her Western mien, raised eyebrows, even in fascist Spain. He ate only rice from the galley, though was seen by a stewardess on the trans-Atlantic hop spooning a murky, green gravy into the widow's tea. The widow never dined.

Back in the baggage hold, Rocket was now more worried when whatever had zombified him would wear off. If he didn't get water soon, he'd go into shock and die.

He didn't have to wait long for wheels-down, and for his body to sense tropical humidity. He heard Vietnamese and French as a human forklift of arms hoisted his coffin out of one baggage hold and into another, this time by arms attached to Chinese bodies, based upon the dialect he could make out.

Kowloon was next. It had to be, because of the distance, the audible Cantonese and English being spoken, along with the noise, smells and traffic. The putt-putt of a boat and rise and fall of swells meant the end was coming. Hong Kong to Canton? Canton to

Shanghai?

Rocket's heartbeats were more rapid, his thirst more painful. He could move his cracked lips. His first weak words when the coffin lid opened and busy underlings fed him herbs and a foul brown tea were, "Kiss my ass..."

*****

The steamy marble bath was fragrant with scented oils. Rocket's belly ached, but somehow his thirst was slaked.

Quickly composed, he fixed on his company: a beefy Chinese man in a white tuxedo shirt and black trousers, pointing a pistol. Abruptly and without a word, the man moved aside...

...and in she strutted, atop high heels, wrapped in a tight black and gold *cheongsam*, dripping with jade and pearls. Nails unsheathed.

"Rocket Crockett," smiled the Shanghai She-Devil in flawless English, looking at his eyes, not his naked form in the water. "No ill effects? I was worried as my powers are on the wane. Time was I could keep someone in living death indefinitely. *Ask my husband.*"

Instinctively, Rocket grabbed for his dog tags. They were gone.

"No-no," giggled the Dowager. "Right here." With a dagger-like nail she lifted the tags; she was wearing them as jewelry. She gestured to a *changshan*, slippers and silk pants on a bench.

After screeching at the guard in Chinese, she whirled and departed, her hips twisting alluringly with each stride.

Dressed and escorted by the goon down a wood-paneled corridor, Rocket heard music, laughter, the clicking of dice, the clacking of mahjong pieces...and roulette numbers called—in Portuguese?

Pigtailed attendants, reminiscent of the *tai pan* colonial days, circled the huge cherrywood table like worker bees, pouring champagne, arranging clay pots of heavenly- scented food.

The Dowager reappeared, licking her black lips.

"Sit, Mr. Crockett. Tonight we have *Galinha*. It's roasted chicken with coconut, curry and potatoes. Specialty of the house." The servants prepared her throne and she sat.

"We're in Macau," mused Rocket as he stepped to the table. A servant pulled out his chair, draped a napkin across his lap and unwrapped a pair of ivory chopsticks. "Shame some regal elephant had to die so I could dine so elegantly. I'll take a knife and fork, thanks."

"Oh, I don't want you anywhere near a knife," laughed the Dowager.

Noticing only a champagne glass in front of his hostess Rocket asked, "All this for me?"

"I dined."

Servants cut pieces of chicken, passed him rice, pickled vegetables, and sauce—all in small bowls. Sampling with the chopsticks, Rocket wasted no time. The food felt good in a stomach unfed for thousands of miles.

The She-Devil fixated on him, wet her lips, crossed her legs.

"I like watching a man eat. His appetite, his manner, his chewing... bespeaks him."

"Viola Jean and the good Reverend Samson, Sr., schooled me well, sister," grinned Rocket after a taste of champagne. "So, why aren't I dead?" He leaned toward her, daunted neither by her menace nor her magnetism.

"I've pretty much burned up, shot up, beat up, messed up or dug up everything important to you. Even heard you want to tie me to a post and cut me."

"Alas, the *lingshi*," sighed the Dowager. "Uttered in fit of womanly spite, I suppose."

She stood, sashayed to the back of his chair, and touched the tips of those nails to his temples, traced his hairline—very, very lightly. He knew she could scalp him if she wished, but he could hear her breathing…felt the brush of ample her bosom on the nape of his neck. She wanted something else.

"So your killing your henchmen, messing up your heroin delivery—all's foregiven?"

"Men can be replaced. And poppies can be replanted. Misery and displacement create infinite supplies of both."

"And that cat, Fan?"

The She-Devil crouched to Rocket's ear, nibbled and kissed it with those black lips. They were strangely rough, not moist, like Mae's.

"I seem to have openings for you to *fill*," she whispered. "Interested?"

Rocket tossed his napkin on the table and turned to face her. "Sister, you must be mainlining your product."

The Dowager laughed contemptuously than commanded, "Come with me…"

Upon more shrill orders from his mistress, the armed goon marched Rocket into a parlor appointed with traditional Chinese furniture, tufted benches, pillows, intricate and old silk painting and carvings. Inexplicably, the henchman departed.

The She-Devil lay on her back on large floor cushions, heels kicked off, stretching from her spine to her bare toes like a cat.

"These paintings are hundreds of years old. But I

recall them as if they were done yesterday. Scenes of my province."

"What is your name?"

"Come here, you dashing fool."

"No."

"You can go to Shanghai as my consort…" warned the Dowager. She flipped over, back arched as her voice went husky, evil. "…or you can go in chains, as my *meat*." And just as quickly, tigress reverted to kitten. "But I don't want the latter. Now…come *here*."

Against every instinct and in fear of loosing his soul, Rocket went to her. He brushed her now-wild hair away from her porcelain-hued face. "I have questions…"

"Hmmm," she purred. "Like 'Why doesn't she sell me to the Reds?'" She looped one leg over Rocket. "I thought of that. But the fools would claim you defected. Not very convincing propaganda after you disappear in a Harlem gang war, eh?"

"Back to the original one. Why am I still alive?"

Rocket unfastened the back of her *cheongsam*, to her appreciative moans.

"As I told you. I have…*openings* you may fill."

"Amen to that."

They kissed. And everything about her was perfumed, soft, intoxicating. Except her lips.

She noted his reticence over that one part of her body, and strangely, it made her instantly coy, almost embarrassed. She could have slaughtered him on the spot. Instead, she turned away.

"So you want to hear my story, now that I have your attention, my warrior from the sky? Well, my name…is *Ting-Zhen*. And I am wife of Dewei Ping, under whose name your 'corpse' traveled. I was betrothed to him when I was fourteen, a year after my girlhood was stolen from me…in the United States of America…on the seventh of April…1869."

She blew Rocket another kiss, and with that breath the floor cushions seemed to sink into a maelstrom, sucking Rocket down as the room whirled above him. In the storm he could feel her warm, wet flesh on his.

Ecstasy and horror formed his mouth into scream, yet he couldn't make a sound as her mouth covered his.

"You will be mine, in Shanghai," he finally heard, through her moans. " Forever. *That* is your punishment, Rocket Crockett."

Chapter 14

Dance of the She-Devil

Rocket massaged his throbbing temples. His clothing, strewn about the parlor, looked as if a predator had shredded them.

He heard a trickle of water. There was full length screen in a corner of the room, near another door. Wondrous silk and woolen embroidery graced its panels. Still, Rocket could see a female form in it, smaller than his evil lover's, yet nude, washing. She sang in a wheezy, broken voice.

Rising as he pulled on what was left of his silk pants, he went to the screen, placed a hand on the frame's edge, craning his neck to look around the corner...

"*Stay away!*" came the husky, inhuman cry. Then, in Chinese, "*Ba bupin, xianzai!*"

He'd only caught a glimpse, and that glimpse froze his heart as he backed away.

Her porcelain skin was jaundiced, dry, specked with moles and splotches. Her luxurious black hair was like gray straw. Her eyes were as yellow as her skin, rimmed in red.

Yet strangely, the lips surrounding those rotted, fanglike teeth were plump, pink, human. Like a young girl's.

Another turtle would have to die and spew its innards before she would face him again.

"We are leaving here," came the voice of a young woman, replenished, as she finally walked around the screen, covered only a long silk robe.

"W-What are you?" begged Rocket, having found plum brandy and downed half the bottle in the interim.

She touched his face but he turned away.

"I swore I would never return to America. I came to see you, for I knew those fools would end up killing you before I had that pleasure. But..." She closed her eyes, "part of me even wanted to see if you could best them, as you bested so many in your war."

Still, he refused to look, and it drew her venom.

"I can *make* you look at me, or tear out your eyeballs in one swipe, you dog!"

"I ain't buying your wolf tickets, lady. Do your worst..."

Rather than attack, she spun away from him, hurt. "*See*? See what you do?"

Flailing him, tasting his blood, would be so easy. But now she wanted only to possess him. That was Rocket's only card, and he was going to play it now matter how it sickened and terrified him.

"You don't understand," shrieked the Dowager. "I came to behold a man who could be my equal. I knew it when I saw your face flutter out of the sky, as if taunting me for the Half Moon Palace. My rage was but a mask, within many sad masks I wear. I've...worn..."

"Oh, so I have to feel sorry for *you*?"

The Dowager howled again, and she ripped the silk robe from her body. No attack came, for she wanted him to see her curse.

Nude, she spun and whirled and dipped and twisted. She danced, enchanting Rocket until he saw, felt, endured...

…an old man, smelling of the white devil's wine and his own filth, buying her from her peasant father for a few French coins and a bag of millet.

Her father had already murdered her mother after seeing what their child could do. His brother—the girl's uncle—tried to touch her. The girl singed manhood with only words, just to defend herself. She didn't even know what she'd done, and begged forgiveness.

On the same quay where Mewo started the chain of events which brought Rocket to the She-Devil's side, were docked the tall ships and steamers flying the flags of the French, British, Austrian, German, Russian dogs chewing at China. There were also the Japanese who wanted their piece. And the Americans. Their ships were the fastest, the tallest.

Each day into Guangzhou and Shanghai poured hundreds of young men from the countryside. They crowded the quay to be voluntary cattle; crammed onto those "clipper" ships with exotic goods for trade.

The cattle was bound for California. There was gold to be pried or coaxed from stone and water. There was a railroad to be built, and it clawed through mountains, laid on desert sands while being vexed by red warriors who rivaled the Mongols in pride and ferocity.

And this human chattel needed women as entertainment, as slaves to the slaves.

She was consigned to the stinking hold of the *Shanghai Scout*, in which stewed smallpox, leprosy, and the filth from groping hands. The dregs spilled into Hawaii, the strongest went to San Francisco, the rest rounded the Horn to New York.

In the streets, old Chinese men picked at her, yelled, checked her teeth. But the women knew what she was, and how her kind might disappear from the family line for generations, then arise. Her power and knowledge of philters and herbs and hexes had to be carefully cultivated, lest she turn to violent witchcraft. Above all, to prevent that turn, her virginity had to remain intact.

But there was no money in keeping her a virgin. First she lay with one of the white sheriffs, toothless and smelly, then some Barbary Coast sailors. She was thirteen. Only afterward was she sold to a work gang as cook, seamstress and concubine.

She followed them from the Sierras, as they erected the same bridge from which Rocket tossed Bert Suh to his death, then to Utah, finally meeting up with the Irish and Negroes pushing rails from the east.

Her power grew—the hexes of drowsiness, visions, and belly sickness came first. Then she developed the ability to rend flesh.

The She-Devil's frenzy slowed to an intricate ballet, and now Rocket saw frightened men who wanted to burn her. *Wupo…sorceress…witch!*

She was saved by a handsome, cocky rail spike-driver named Dewei Zhou Ping who *never* averted his eyes from white bosses.

He was ambitious: earning their money, cutting his pigtail, and dressing the part. And when he'd had enough of the whites, he took her as a child bride on this new railroad, east to New York, with trinkets and baubles and herbs from China in tow.

With her hexes and her love, he built a prosperous business in Chinese dry goods, loaned money to other Chinese, and dealt in vice. He hired thugs to protect that business. He joined with the ancient Orchid Tong back home. The die was cast…until he bid her to teach him her dark art.

"I will no longer be dependent on a teenage whore,"

he told his tong.

That betrayal spelled his doom. Some say he lay under her palace in Shanghai, in the 20th century, dead yet alive and aware, for no one actually saw the body of Dewei Zhou Ping after he took sick.

He became a legend, a chimera, a front for her rule. "David Chow" to Americans—founder of the Wing Fat Sino-American Trading Company. He was said to have returned home to China to claim his throne as Father Blossom of the Orchid Tong, and, in his old age, took a young, ruthless bride.

Dance done, she collapsed, naked and sweating at Rocket's bare feet.

"There's no child. No one, onto whom I can pass my rule. So I had no choice but to live on. I drink the boiled bile and blood of *Shénshèng de wūguī* as it dies, so I may live. I become dangerous and crave the shedding of human blood…to calm my own."

She slinked onto his lap, pulling a cotton cover up around them both, as if Rocket was her protector, not her prey.

"But the hex stains the lips," whispered the Dowager, with eternal regret. "And you will not want to kiss them ever again."

"When do we leave?" muttered Rocket, unsure in his soul whether was playing his card, or bewitched?

"Tomorrow, sunrise. Less trouble from the Reds along the coast."

"That dance," he whispered, "don't ever do it again."

"Only if you promise never to look at me, as *time* sees me, ever again."

He nodded, and prayed for the dawn as they made love.

Chapter 15

Danger is His Trade

In the lair of the She-Devil, a week seemed like months. Yet back in the world, ONI and the CIA kept Rocket's disappearance close the vest. The New York newspapers mentioned a gang battle-royal over dope, but nothing of Rufus Crockett. Witnesses like DeWitt got visits from ONI in the hospital or were whisked to Washington and held *in communicato*. So the witnesses stayed quiet.

Only Julie Wang, her father and aunt, and Bonelip had any inkling where Rocket might be, since his body was not in the Hudson River floating next to White Paper Fan.

All Auntie Ming could utter was the odd word *wupo* –"witch"—as the g-men, Navy men and CIA lickspittles interrogated her.

The cops took ten pounds of uncut China White out of the rotted floor of that coal building. And then the dope disappeared soon after it was seized. Law enforcement would never find it again, though would resurface, making bad times worse, after another war in the east.

As for Bonelip Broussard, he was a Catholic and thus on his knees in the dingy chapel at the Brooklyn Navy Yard, entreated God to give Rocket strength and perseverance wherever he was.

"Lawd, I know de boy doin' whateva he gotta do ta stay alive. Tell him I saved his bat...an' tell him we comin'."

Later, the Kuomintang Nationalists on the island of Formosa would send angry dispatches to the U.S. Seventh Fleet, demanding to know why the USS *Bonhomme Richard* and two destroyers were suddenly sent to the island of Okinawa. They moaned that would leave Taiwan open to incursions by its Communist enemy. The Navy ignored the messages...

And so, as Bonelip continued his vigil, a junk that looked so ordinary on the outside, and so luxurious on the inside, slid into the Yangtze delta with the evening tide, then down the Huangpu River.

Two black Renault sedans took off with the disembarked passengers—bodyguards, servants and two figures who were hooded, and shrouded, all under the noses of wandering Commie guards. The cars were followed by a truck. Rocket caught a whiff of the cargo. Not processed morphine from the fecund womb of the poppy, but rather something just as important: ether, to transform it into China White.

The cars and truck cut and zig-zagged into the slums until they passed through an open iron gate and into a courtyard fronting a huge house that resembled a regal pagodas of old. The truck detoured to an attached garage to offload the volatile chemical.

"Ahhh, home!" trilled the Dowager, seemingly happy for the first time in decades.

Rocket entered the house through a great hall lit by candles and scented by incense.

"Don't ever step there," gestured the She-Devil, as Rocket felt the floor creak below a set of bamboo steps. He moved as she climbed stairs, shifted her weight and smiled.

The floor opened up and a foul smell wafted into the

hall. Sewer gas, death. Rocket looked down. Ugly iron spikes stared back up at him.

"Impressive," admitted the newly-consecrated colored consort. "Magic?"

"No," giggled the Dowager, almost giddy. "Mere mechanics. Follow me my love."

Finally, she had a man of mythic prowess, worthy of seeing a vestige of her age. She led him to the glass case, in which the treasure displayed on a woven reed mannequin.

It was a *chaofu* robe, green as hers, yet embroidered with horses, wagons, goods, swords, and crossbows. A cylindrical *Jinxianguan* crown rested on the mannequin's head.

"This is the garment of—"

"Warrior-poets and merchant nobles," finished Rocket, recalling a dim memory of a romantic literature lecture at Howard.

She wasn't used to being interrupted. For an instant, her eyes flashed, yet his impertinence, his love of danger, remained endearing.

"It was the plundered possession a corrupt warlord," said the Dowage. "Dewei had him liquidated and the gown liberated. He shipped it to America to adorn himself when we renewed our wedding vows, in splendor, far from the cesspool camps, steel rails and Indians." She closed her eyes. "July 16, 1883, in the Wing Fat Hall on Mott Street. Our garments are two thousand years old." She opened her eyes, stitching her gaze on Rocket. "I wear mine when I hold court over the captains of the Orchid Tong…my wedding gown."

"Oh boy," Rocket whispered with a shudder.

"You will wear this, as the *new* Father Blossom. And we shall rebuild. My recompense, restitution, my *new* dowry…is your heart and soul."

Rocket's heart fluttered against his sternum.

"I'm…I'm, honored."

"You should be."

"But, don't take this the wrong way. I can't be your man unless I have assurances I won't end up like a boy spider, or a boy mantis, you dig?"

This impertinence she couldn't laugh off. She rushed to him, pressing her claws into his throat, black lips curled.

Rocket didn't flinch, he didn't wince. "You can't help yourself, can you, baby? I'm a slave…your *meat*. Not your man. You'll never treat me as an equal."

Withdrawing her nails, she sighed heavily and snapped, "Assurances, eh? Like what?"

Rocket lifted her chin. He braved another kiss on those cold, dead lips. Her tongue, however, was hot.

"I don't want to learn how you do what you," uttered Rocket between hungry kisses. "That's how your first husband betrayed you. But I want to see these terrapins you keep, like the dames back home hoard cold cream."

"Ha!" joked the Dowager. "Like you hoard that hair slop? Bah! I have ointments that will make your hair straight as a Chinese man's, and never fall out."

"You could make a fortune off of colored folk with that. But, may I remind you that without Smoov Mallard, there'd be no me and you, baby."

"Come."

As an arid night wind from the west displaced the muggy breezes from the south, the couple strolled through another airy hall to a courtyard strung with buzzing hot electrical lamps and guarded by a servant. Hundred of turtles swam and waddled in marble pools.

"Beautiful," noted Rocket. "I suppose the lamps

come on at night, to warm them?"

The Shanghai She-Devil nodded.

It was then Rocket noticed a tunnel housing the water pipe that fed the pools. From it he caught the faint smell of ether.

"Time for sleep," prompted the bride-to-be. "Much to do: bribes to the Communist imbeciles in Beijing and Chiang's fools across the strait in Taipei. You, Rufus Crockett, shall be my brains as White Paper Fan was. Help me deal with this day-to-day."

"Okey-doke."

Laughing at his Americanism she added, "You need a decent Tong name."

To Rocket's surprise, she slept like a rock, sawing more wood than a dozen exhausted swabbies on *Bonhomme Richard*. Such was the toll of energy taken to keep herself beautiful.

Accordingly, for the first time in his captivity, he was able to roam free of her clutches. Though the eunuch-like retainers never spoke, they entertained his every request, even late into the night.

Tonight his request was "drink." He wanted the strongest booze they could lay their hands on.

They brought it before morning: bottles of British gin mixed with a colorless Chinese liquor flavored with cardamom, cinnamon and herbs.

The Dowager woke at dawn yet didn't seem to mind his cache.

"But if you become a drunkard," warned his mistress, combing her hair in a wall mirror and with some playfulness in her voice, "I shall have to kill you."

A kiss assuaged her, and she went to do her business in the ageless gown.

Alone, searching the blue sky and clouds where he

ruled in the Typewriter, Rocket pondered his options. Even if he could jump the wall and surrender to the first Commie grunt toting a *PePeSha*—or beat feet to the same Russian Legation he'd papered with leaflets a month ago—he figured they'd just turn him back over to her, and she'd murder him and all he loved back home. The Swiss Legation was across town. No way he'd make it.

"No one's coming," mulled Rocket, aloud. "So I would rather *end* this, and break rocks in a Red POW camp when the smoldering ashes cool, than be her pet."

When White Paper Fan failed to return from his mysterious mission, Orchid soldiers feared ferment at the top and weakness exposed to the other tongs. But the reappearance of their Mother Blossom that morning steeled them, and with her came the news of a consort. The wedding would symbolize renewal: the poppy juice flowing north again, the money counted, the power enjoyed.

Before the wedding, the tong planned a feast for local Communist Party officials bought with graft and favors. Fireworks would proclaim the moment when the Mother Blossom would no longer be a dowager. The gangsters promised that the display of light and fire would surpass even that seen over the city to celebrate the surrender of Japan in 1945!

As the feast commenced and the rockets were primed, the Mother Blossom invaded Rocket's wardrobe room, wearing no more than a dressing gown and high-heeled slippers, puffing on her cigarette holder. Servants were busy pinning and wrapping Rocket in his ancient *chaofu*, while another toady painted the make-up of a noble warrior groom on his face.

"In America its bad luck to see the bride before the

wedding," quipped Rocket, as his face was brushed white.

"This isn't America," she giggled.

"Isn't this a little risky...me, here, with two dozen Reds downstairs? Not every Commie, just like not every Kuomintang chief, is on the take. They *will* find out I'm here."

Rocket was reaching, but it was worth a try. She dismissed the servants.

"I thought we discussed this, Rufus Crockett. You are of limited propaganda value now."

"I'm sorry. Just, ya know...jitters about going down the aisle, eh? Lotta dames have tried to catch me. Man, imagine how cranky they'll be when they find out the winner of the Rocket Sweepstakes is a Chinese sorceress."

"I am just a woman. Has anyone come close to being your wife?"

He shrugged, which was difficult to do with the extra pounds of silk, cotton, wool, beads and jade.

"Good," huffed the bride-to-be. "As it must be."

Before she could summon the servants, Rocket looked to the *Jinxianguan* crown now perched on a pillow.

"Even with Smoov Mallard, that's not gonna stick to my noggin. I don't have a horse tail of your 'good hair' to pin that in."

"Hmmm, you are correct. They will think of something."

"Gimme a minute...I'm an engineer, too. And...I have to hit the head..."

"My funny husband," cooed the She-Devil as she floated from the room.

The wicks were made of shredded cotton and melted

candlewax, with incense he'd pilfered. He'd positioned them during what the guards and servants believed to be a nocturnal drunken tour. A string of sputtering hot lights made a wonderful timing fuse. They just had to be switched on. And the liquor, once ignited, would to sucking enough air from that tunnel to pull in the ether from the processing lab…

Under the gown, he'd hidden the decanters of liquor that he would have to plant. It wasn't hard to pull his arms out of the *chaofu*'s great fluted sleeves and reach toward his body. Rocket ambled out, looking like a float in his own parade.

As he predicted, but for his own body servants and whomever was dressing his blushing bride, the rest of the flunkies had adjourned to the great hall. Though weighed down by his costume, Rocket set up his sabotage devices.

Miraculously, he made it back, pantomiming a bathroom break as the excuse to the bewildered servants, who had to repaint the makeup he'd sweated off his face.

I'm not a bad man, Rocket mulled as they adjusted the crown. *Just a dangerous one*.

CHAPTER 16

POP GOES THE WEASEL

A robed priest escorted Rocket down the bamboo stairs to face the assembled thuggery. Rocket had always envisioned Bonelip as his best man; this certainly wasn't Brenda about to come down the aisle.

The priest chanted Daoist verse and other canticles Rocket could barely understand with his limited Mandarin.

"All glory, pearls, ivory, jade and coin to the Orchid Tong

Long life to Father Blossom!"

"Long life to Father Blossom!" thundered their reply.

Several flutes, *tiqin* fiddles , cymbals, and drums kept harmony and rhythm with an eerie, yet beautiful melody led by a *pipa* lute and a zither.

"Here comes the bride," Rocket sang, to calm himself.

The Mother Blossom entered the hall, flanked two servants dressed in eunuch finery.

Rocket met her on the floor panel that opened up into oblivion, and nervously watched the expounding and bloviating priest sway and bounce on the trigger step.

Noting her groom's unease, the bride winked at him.

Upon a final chant from the officiate, the bride presented him with a badge of office: a white paper fan.

Rocket bowed to his new wife. It was then he saw her

nod to one of the pigtailed servants, and Rocket prayed the toady was heading where he hoped. After all, the ole ball 'n chain was likely getting hungry.

Upon her command, a group of hoodlums departed in the opposite direction. They'd already dismissed the Red dignitaries; some were preparing the fireworks while others went to the courtyard.

Through the open panels of the hall, Rocket spotted an idling car waiting outside. The thugs returned with a human-sized, writhing burlap sack.

Ting-Zhen Crockett, no longer a dowager, ordered the sack forward, perilously close to the trap door floor. A goon cut the fabric. Rocket gasped.

The hair was different, the clothes were drab, tattered. But she had almost the same face as Julie Wang, of Harlem.

"Regrettably," announced Ting-Zhen in her husband's tongue, "she was located too late to affect the outcome in New York. And sadly, for her, she refused the gift of her defiler's severed instruments of defilement. I did not even have the satisfaction of such revenge. So tonight, her blood will be the cement of our bond, my love."

As Mewo cowered and squirmed in the guard's grasp, Rocket muttered, "So she was the one who wanted me to rescue her family…" he turned to his wife. "…from *you.*"

Jutting her lovely chin, Ting-Zhen snapped, "And so the loop closes…and you are my family now."

She ordered the goons to move away from a whimpering Mewo, and commanded the priest off of the trigger stair.

Rocket sucked in a breath and prayed to a God with whom he rarely conversed, as the Mother Blossom moved closer to that deadly step.

It was time.

Knocking off his *Jinxianguan* crown, the Father Blossom shouted: Mewo! *Tiàole!*

At first, the girl was stunned motionless, but as the floor opened, she managed to fall away from its evil maw.

Before his wife could react, Rocket seized the priest and flung him off the stairs. Like a seven pin hitting the ten, he took a surprised, pistol-wielding henchman onto the hungry spikes with him.

Now Rocket faced the full rage of the She-Devil. Her back arched, her black lips parted, her white teeth flashed.

"*You!*" shrieked the once frightened, abused teenage girl, turned witch and monster.

She uttered a hex, and lifted her nails to strike.

Suddenly, a shockwave of hot, acrid air blasted down the stairs, carrying with it a screaming servant engulfed in flame, his flesh crisping.

He'd flicked the switch to the lights that warmed the turtles, activating Rocket's improvised Molotov cocktails… and the carelessly unharnessed vapor of gallons of ether…

The smell of the turtles' burnt flesh tinged Ting-Zhen's nostrils before that of her suffering retainer's. And strangely, her rage evaporated. Not into panic, or terror, but rather, despair.

Thick black smoke billowed through the pagoda-like palace almost instantly, sending Orchids scurrying aimlessly, like ants without a queen.

And so the claws didn't rend or rip at Rocket, who by now was struggling to peel off as many layers of the two thousand-year-old-garment as possible. Instead, they clutched at him, in anguish.

"*W-Why?*"

"Something my people learned, the hard way, also in the holds of ships. You don't avenge being a slave…by making slaves of others."

She spun away from him, wailing , as a guard swung a sword. The *chaofu* absorbed the blow as Rocket pivoted and then landed a cross chop to the man's throat.

Still, even in the confusion and smoke, a few goons managed to get a line of sight on Rocket, glowing in his robe. They aimed their pistols.

"I guess we go out together," whispered Rocket to an unseen Ting-Zhen.

The rounds never fired, for a pineapple grenade landed among them, splattering them all over the great hall a split second later.

The fireworks masked the sound of submachine gun fire as several men dressed in green battle fatigues, faces painted black, invaded the space.

Even through the face paint, one of the commandoes recognized Rocket. The figure lunged through the smoke, grabbing Rocket off the stairs.

Rocket took cover from the gunfire behind an overturned carved bench. Another figure in green dragged Mewo to safety.

And then he felt a hand clutch his own. Despite the glove, Rocket could tell the hand didn't belong to a man.

"Your honeymoon's been cancelled, *flyboy*!" boasted Mae Tanaka, through the black camouflage make-up.

"What kept ya?"

"We've only got a few minutes!" shouted Mae over the pandemonium. "Thank you for the diversion but we had enough plastique to destroy the processing lab."

"Are you kidding me?" grunted Rocket, rising with her. " You're *my* diversion.

Suddenly, Rocket felt something hook onto his back, climbing, clawing, as if a wild animal.

He whipped around to see a hand with long fingernails swiping, stabbing. Both the hand and the arm attached to it were wrinkled, the flesh mottled. The attack drew blood, yet had little force behind it.

As Mae watched in horror, Rocket sloughed off a shell of a woman. Her hair was straw-like and matted. Her eyes were beady, hooded, red. The creature could barely hold the form of its once beauteous green costume; pearl and jade earrings pulled and distorted the ears.

"I-I hate you," spit the hag through lips as tender and innocent as a thirteen- year-old girl's. And then, in a whisper, "I…loved…you…"

"Mae," gulped Rocket, his own lips aquiver, "let's blow…"

He wriggled out of the gown as embers fluttered like fiery butterflies.

Ting-Zhen leapt with whatever life was left in her old body, claws extended to kill.

Mae emptied the entire clip from her .45 into the Shanghai She-Devil. But it was Rocket Crockett who killed her.

*****

Rocket was silent and brooding as he joined the company of men shooting their way to the waiting 1930's vintage Ford trucks. They'd been reconditioned by the Chinese and looked like any moving through the streets of Shanghai, even after curfew.

Soon the horizon glowed from fire. More rockets exploded into bright blossoms of color. The irony wasn't lost on Rocket, as he watched Mewo bawling, rattled, but grateful. As the trucks rumbled past unsuspecting Red soldiers more interested in the fireworks, Mewo cried for her little brother and sister, for it seemed they'd be left behind.

A commando stripped off his gear and shirt, and wiped his face clean. Under the black camouflage paint, he was Chinese. He assured her no one was leaving them, for her family in Harlem told ONI exactly where the children lived in Shanghai.

Rocket watched, amazed, as all of them, Mae included, stripped, wiped their faces and pulled on homespun coolie shirts or dingy *changsans*. Most in the truck were Chinese, a few looked Korean.

"Army? USMC? Navy Combat Demolition?" pressed Rocket to the man comforting Mewo.

"At one point, sir, yes. For this, we're CIA. Sino-American Scouts. Jack Kwan is in the other truck; he surveyed this entire coastline when the Chinese were fighting the Japs," he paused, looking to Mae. "No offense, ma'am."

"None taken," intoned Mae, wrapping her hair in a kerchief. "We fetch the kids," she told Rocket, "head for the sampans we stashed and pray we miss the 'dragon tide' coming back in... and that the patrol boats aren't trawling.

"To where?"

Mae planted a wet kiss on Rocket's lips. A human kiss. "You've been 'round and 'round the mulberry bush, flyboy, so don't worry your handsome head about it."

"Pop goes the weasel," laughed Rocket.

Chapter 17

Out of the Frying Pan

By dawn the Reds were neither distracted by, nor preoccupied with, the She-Devil's burning palace. They'd found the spent rounds and dropped gear in the ruins and ashes, and realized they'd been invaded.

Bodies, both shot-up and charred, were collected, and the surviving gangsters were rounded up for re-education camps or conscription. Like Uncle Sam, the commies wanted to erase their flirtation with dope... at least for now.

An informer told them that some supply trucks had driven into impoverished Chaingnang district stopping only once before mysteriously, then taking off north to the junction of the Yangtze and Huanpo. There were men in the truck. Laborers. What were laborers doing in two precious trucks needed by the army?

With all forces engaged, the local commander left one commissar behind to pick through the smoldering remains of the house. The officer was a petite, bespectacled young woman with a mop of black hair stuffed under her drab green field cap.

Under a fallen beam she found a treasure, damaged slightly, yet untouched by the fire or bullets. Once trained as a history teacher before the Great Victory, she knew immediately what she'd discovered: the outer wrap of a nobleman's gown. A *chaofu* of great age and immense value. It was perhaps post-Han Dynasty, early Jin…

Something else caught her eyes as she hurriedly scribbled in her note pad. She touched it with her pencil. It looked like fabric: green, intricate and still supple. She gasped as she lifted it with her free hand. The fire hadn't touched it but it still was fouled by soot.

Gingerly, she gathered the fabric, but dropped it, heaving air when she heard a rattling sound inside. A skinless wrist, radius and ulna poked out from one of the sleeves. The craggily digits ending in long fingernails, still varnished red.

Quaking, she brushed away more soot and debris. A skull appeared, with dry, dead hair still attached to the remnants of its leathery scalp. The eyes were crusted, rotted out. The jaw was shut. Around the cervical vertebrae however, was something modern. A chain. American dog-tags?

She covered her mouth, unable to speak, or vomit. This woman had not died in the fire. And so with the flat end of pencil she lifted off the dog-tags, pocketed them, crouched closer to poke at the skull.

The jaw opened. A rush of hot wind captured ashand flecks of remaining flesh, as if the skull blew it last breath…

…right into the commissar's mouth.

She doubled over, coughing, swallowing, spitting, wheezing. The minute she felt composed, the seizures hit her. Her head and heart burned. And soon, she danced…

*****

Two motorized sampans buffered with old auto tires puttered in tandem beyond the wide mouth and pale yellow waters of the delta, past curious fisherman and hurrying tradesmen.

Rocket, his face obscured by the conical bamboo *dŏulì* on his head, tried to calm Mewo's young siblings. She had to ride in the other sampan to make the passengers look like a group of workers ferrying themselves to a junk anchored far out into the East China Sea for a journey south. Anchored so far, in fact, it likely violated the Red ordinances to that effect, and the fishermen and tradesmen warned them sternly, to no avail.

With a pair of binoculars, one of the Sino-American Scouts spotted the mother vessel bobbing in the distant white caps. Rocket took a look. It was a two-masted junk, though oddly shaped.

"That canoe ain't gonna outrun a patrol boat, fellas."

"We've modified it, Lieutenant…"

As if on devilish cue, everyone in both boats turned their heads to the distant sounds of sirens. Rocket aimed the binoculars. Two Red patrol boats, packed with soldiers, were bearing down on them.

"Ahoy!" Rocket shouted to Mae's boat, "Get some speed up! It's a horserace now!"

Worse news came off the port bow, even more distant than the junk. Rocket focused the glasses. It was a minesweeper, its red flag fluttering from the radio masthead. A pugnacious 3-inch fifty-caliber gun swiveled on the deck.

"Out of the frying pan…" groaned Rocket to one of the commandoes. "Our only hope is that the minesweeper's skipper is a dumbass gomer and turns onto our heading. Otherwise, if he knows that's the mothership, he can stand off and blow her to bits and we might as well stop."

Rocket signaled the man operating the other sampan's outboard to make some wide turns and feign divergent courses. It might draw the minesweeper into an intercept path, but it also meant the patrol boats would catch up faster.

As the yellow water under the sampans turned blue and choppy, Rocket aimed the binoculars to spy a sign of hope: the minesweeper's single funnel puffed black smoke, and the bow started to turn.

The hope was short-lived as the patrol boats unleashed barrages of machine gun fire. The rounds were falling short, but they had the desired effect: fear. The children screamed, Mewo sank her head, and the men and Mae stared grimly. Yet still the distance between the junk and the lowly sampans closed with each agonizing, sea-sprayed second, and the larger ship seemed decoyed away.

Refugees must have attempted to flee the mainland in suicidally-small boats before, avoiding the tsunami-like dragon tide and hitting the open sea. So the commies weren't stupid, Rocket now surmised. This maneuver was simply standard operating procedure.

"Bring us together!" shouted Rocket over the gunfire, engine whirr and crashing waves. "Straight for the junk again. Hell bent for leather!"

One of the Sino-American commandoes pulled out a walkie talkie. "Charlie Bravo this is Charlie Expedition… coming in hot. Get those engines revving, over."

"Way ahead of you, come in on starboard side net even if we have to tow you, over."

"Please tell me y'all have an ace up your sleeves," prodded Rocket.

Mae's sampan reached the junk just as the patrol boats' fire was piercing the water; they were even in range of the assault rifles and *PePeShas* carried by the onboard soldiers. Out of the sampan and up the cargo nets, spiderlike, went Mae and her men, pushing a frantic

Mewo up and over.

Rocket's boat slid in next, and it was then Rocket heard, then saw, the ace up the sleeve.

This was no junk. The hull rumbled with Detroit engines. The barnacled planks camouflaged a PT boat.

Fighting off pleas to go first, Rocket helped each man up the netting until he, alone, was in the sampan.

The PT boat started to move. Rocket's hands were on the lines, but his feet were still in the sampan. That's when the first shells from the minesweeper whistled and crashed into the water barely a hundred yards off the starboard beam. A line of machine gun fire from the pursuing patrol boats raked the netting, and Mae screamed as Rocket fell back into the sampan.

But the PT had another surprise. Crewmen tore off the bow camouflage to reveal a twin 40mm Bofors gun. The weapon opened up on the minesweeper. Another shell splashed even closer before the Bofors gave the Red sailors pause.

Still, the attacker had the range. All they needed was one hit…

The PT boat turned with Rocket's arms on the net as the only thing tethering the sampan. Commandoes firing their carbines from the deck didn't scare off the patrol boats, now so close Rocket could hear the soldiers on shouting at each other.

Mae, eyes wild and tearing, shouted frantically to the boat's skipper, who likewise wore no discernible uniform or rank, "We need thirty seconds dammit!"

Dodging rounds from the patrol boats, she grabbed a cylindrical object from a wounded commando. "Jump, Rocket!"cried Mae as she raised and leveled the tube. It was a bazooka, and the girl had but one shot.

Rocket leaped for the net. The PT boat's engines

pushed the craft in a mighty surge.

"Clear!" shouted Mae, hoarse. She fired. The projectile missed the first target but it found the second one. That boat exploded in fire, its crew jumping for their lives.

The PT boat roared ahead at full speed, with Rocket as a human water ski.

With that much force, it was impossible to lift him out, and the craft dared not slow. Still, they were opening the distance between the minesweeper's gun and freedom.

Gulping seawater, exhausted, and pounded against the hull, Rocket still held on. *I come through too much mess to die in the ocean!*

After a few tense minutes, the minesweeper and smoke from the exploded patrol boat were small on the western horizon. With the PT boat at full speed, skimming the waves of the East China Sea, the crewmen and commandoes decided it was now or never. They were able to lower a looped line to Rocket, just as his strength gave out.

"Heave!" they called in unison.

They'd nearly gotten him over the gunwales to cheers and shouts of joy when the skipper popped off the bridge, pointing skyward. Though battered, Rocket looked up, too.

It was a flight of Yak-9s in echelon and about to dive on the PT boat.

"...and into the fire," whispered Rocket.

Mae ushered Rocket onto the open bridge and slapped a wool blanket on him.

"Baby," panted Rocket, "we outta aces?"

Just as the Yaks were about to make their strafing run, the radio crackled with a familiar voice: "Charlie Bravo...this is Tomcat Delta Echo, Strike Squadron 25, stand-by…"

When the first Yaks exploded in mid-air and the rest winged off, willy nilly, Rocket tossed back his head did something he hadn't done since the She-Devil shanghaied him—something hadn't done since he sojourned to Harlem, or crossed the continent on a train. In fact, he couldn't remember the last time he'd done it. Nearly doubling over, he erupted with a carefree belly-laugh!

"St. Anselmo, you *guinea!*" chortled Rocket, saluting a sky now buzzing with banjos.

In a few minutes, the PT boat met picketing destroyers out of Okinawa. And beyond that screen steamed the Goodtime Dickie.

Neither the squadron nor the crew, other than Captain Connor, was allowed to know what the mission was, or who, if anyone, was extracted. All they knew was that their prodigal, proud , pugnacious and a shade lighter than piceous son was coming home to them after he recovered from an "auto accident in Harlem, New York."

CHAPTER 18

ROCKET CROCKETT, HE'S OUR MAN

The taxi turned off 4th Street onto T. Rocket climbed out, still nursing a limp and sore ribs. He carried a bouquet of pink dahlias and yellow daisies in one white-gloved hand, a baseball bat wrapped in a red ribbon in the other.

The stand collar of dress white tunic, and brass buttons fixed almost up to his chin chafed all the way through the ceremony, but after everything Rocket had been through, that was almost like a tickle.

Besides, getting the cable from Brenda Goins that she was so happy to hear Rocket was back in Washington, instructing him to please hurry over at his earliest convenience, made up for the morning's real sting.

What stung was being there at the Pentagon to watch Captain Connor get his star from Arleigh Burke, after Burke got a second one from Admiral Forrest Sherman, then Connor pinned a gold eagle on Commander— now Captain—Hollins and handed him command of *Bonhomme Richard* .

None of them, save Sherman and an absent Commander Harry Abensour, knew that Rocket had broken the back of the China White trade in Harlem. Or that Rocket suffered as male concubine to the Shanghai She-Devil in her lair.

Even Abensour didn't believe him—as if the power

of Jade Dragon had been equally plausible, or the witchcraft of counter-espionage was somehow concrete and laudable?

In the end, it was the usual suspects who were the ones being celebrated, feted, rewarded, and retired. So Rocket dutifully stood at attention, mouth shut, sword at his side, in the second row of officers, unmentioned and barely noticed beyond the usual gawks he got as if he indeed was the mythical unicorn. A few intrepid civilians and officers' wives did shake his hand, however, as "the colored aviator who saved Ted Williams."

When the ceremony ended, the senior brass went across the Potomac for cocktails and roast beef at the Army-Navy Club on Farragut Square. The only officer below the rank of captain invited to the party was Ensign F. Grayson Morse, Jr.

The others decided to unwind in a joint close by in Alexandria,. It was Jim Crow, so Rocket wasn't welcome, and even Mario St. Anselmo asked him to be a good sport.

"You and I both know there're plenty of colored places in town that are a lot more fun, Rufus! Hell, you usually can't wait to cut us loose, so why the long face?"

Indeed.

Those gray thoughts dissolved when Brenda opened the door, beaming. Her ubiquitous pearls glowed against a red blouse. Her hair was perfect, as was her face, her legs, her shoes—so much so that the simple apron she wore looked comically inapt to that elegance.

Brenda looked Rocket up and down. Yes, he made good on his promise to wear his dress whites next time he saw her. He even had a sword, bless his heart!

She kissed his cheek.

He felt a little uneasy, tucking the bat under his arm

and crossing the threshold as he removed his hat. This was Dr. Goins' house, after all.

But then he sniffed roast chicken, the gooey golden treasure of baked macaroni and cheese, a hint of collard greens. A peach cobbler cooled on console table in the hall.

Yet as Rocket passed the dining room, he noticed the table set for five: one seat stacked with phone books for the older boy, a metal high chair for the tot…and three for adults.

"Rufus these flowers are divine," gushed Brenda. "Lemme put them in water. " She winked, pointing at the bat. "And *that* is for my sons? They will hardly lift that together!"

"I'll teach 'em," grinned Rocket. "It's autographed by Willie Mays and Jackie Robinson. This thing's been through a lot."

"As have you?" sighed Brenda.

"One day soon, I'll tell you."

He tried to move closer to her but she threw up her hands playfully and insisted the bird needed last-minute tending.

"Make yourself at home in the living room. Matter of fact the boys are watching baseball for the first time ever on a television. Giants and Dodgers! Fate, eh?"

"Yes ma'am," affirmed Rocket. "Giants can force a playoff. All was lost a month ago. Now, triumph. So yeah…fate. I now believe in it wholeheartedly, Brenda. *Wholeheartedly.*"

He walked to the living room with the bat as she asked how Bonelip was doing.

"In port in San Diego until we biggity officers come back and—"

Rocket quieted when he rounded the corner, expecting

to see two children on the floor enjoying a game. They were.

And also, lounging on the sofa, was a gentleman with Rocket's thin mustache, laid-down and shiny hair, wearing razor-creased slacks, spotless brown oxfords, a gray cardigan and plum tie. He was more into Pee Wee Reese's base hit on the glowing screen than noticing Rocket.

That's until Brenda's older son shouted, "Wow, it's the Navy man!"

The tot mimicked, "Wow" and pointed to the bat.

The gentleman crushed out his cigarette on the coffee table ashtray, jumped to his feet and inflated his chest as quickly as Rocket's deflated.

"Osborne Jefferson!" exclaimed interloper yanking at Rocket's hand. "Thrilled to meet you, man. Brenda's just over the moon that you came."

"Rufus Crockett," muttered Rocket.

"Uh-huh, the 'Rocket!' Well you can call me 'Oz' as all my friends do. Saaaay…whatcha got there?" He snatched the bat from Rocket's limp hand. "Boss autographs! But you know who I had the pleasure of talking with the other day? Adlai Stevenson. And I arranged a conference for a bright young lawyer by the name of Robert Kennedy. He's gonna be something, watch. Ya know, his brother John's a Navy hero, like you."

Brenda hurried in to defuse and buffer. "Oz is the first colored day manager at the Mayflower Hotel. Greets the luminaries. Frank-Junior, if you've washed you hands, go and help your brother get seated."

The little fellows scampered out. Brenda crouched to switch off the set.

"Doll, it's the bottom of the eighth," whined Oz.

"Dodgers have men on base."

"Oh g'won and help them get settled," huffed Brenda. "You can bless the table."

Oz strode out, leaving Brenda searching her feet, and Rocket floating, as if a specter.

"I-I'm sorry, Rufus," whispered Brenda. "He's the brother of one my girlfriends at work. He's very nice… the boys love him."

"That was quick. Funeral was when, remind me?"

This time she did draw close. "Don't, Rufus. *Don't*. We are friends. We have meals, go dancing. We've been to movies. That's it. He is a perfect gentleman."

"He loves you."

"That's my business. I don't ask you who *your* latest conquest has been. Some chippie up in Harlem, or doe-eyed little country gal back in Memphis?"

A million images, horrific and sublime, almost short-circuited Rocket's brain in the instant it took them to pass across his mind's eyes. He almost mumbled about *Michiko-san* in Tokyo, or Mae, just to hurt her. But the images ceased with a flash: a succubus's eyes, her intoxicating body.

"*Yeah*," snapped Rocket. "Conquest? Her name was Ting-Zhen. *She was my wife*. I watched her *die*. You happy now?"

Brenda was frozen in place as Oz and the boys, utterly oblivious, requested her presence.

"R-Rufus…what?"

"We don't really know a damn thing about each other anymore, do we? Did we ever? We were kids. Floating on a fun, phony raft called college. I gotta go…"

He moved past her and stormed to the door of the tidy rowhouse. For a second, Brenda hesitated, then gave chase, catching his arm in full view of Oz.

"Doll?" called Oz, eyebrow arched. "Everything cool?"

"Sit, Oz. Rufus just…recalled he may have dropped his glove outside, is all."

"Don't blame me for running out on you this time."

"Stay."

"No games, Brenda."

"No, please. Stay, eat and, be nice…and then we can—"

The door bell rang. Oz shot up as if he were the man of the house, and Rocket glowered at him for it.

Brenda opened the door. Two white men in gray suits, gray hats with gold lapel pins stood with derisive looks on their faces, as if they were the ones being inconvenienced.

"Brenda Marie LeBeau Goins?" huffed one of them while the other eyed Rocket. He took out a small memo book and scribbled, noting Oz as well.

"Um yes, is there a problem?" quizzed Brenda, clutching her pearl necklace.

He handed her a piece of paper backed in blue. "If you attempt to evade the requests of this document, you will be arrested by the FBI and your children placed in colored foster care…"

They had bounded down to a waiting car beyond the gate before Oz gave chase like a dutiful mutt.

Speechless, Brenda sank back in the doorway. Rocket took the paper and read the word "Subpoena." It wasn't until he got to the middle of the page that he fixated on the words "House Un-American Activities Committee." It was signed by The Hon. Richard M. Nixon, California, on behalf of the Chairman, The Hon. F. Grayson Morse, Sr., Ohio...

Morse.

Rocket folded the subpoena into his uniform pocket. With a smile and a reassuring grip on Brenda's shoulder while she showed a brave face to her sons, he said, "Baby…send the little dog out there home. The big dog is here."

"But you're shipping out…"

"Uh-huh. But I'll be back. After typing… *tap-tap-tap* …a new story of adventure and daring. And ain't nobody going to mess with you or your family then, 'cause I got many stories. Some a few folk might be scared of."

Almost as reflex, Brenda shut the door. Oz was outside, ringing the bell, knocking, as she served the chicken, spooned the gooey macaroni and portioned the collards. Rocket said grace.

"Aw *come on*, doll!" pleaded the hapless suitor, banished to the sidewalk. "Listen…did the Dodgers win, at least?"

So, as a warm, bright September congealed into a cool, murky October, the Korean War scribed yet another bloody chapter in the book of death. Some of that crimson ink was spilled by Lt. Rufus "Rocket" Crockett, USN, blasting his name into the manuscript from the slums of Shanghai to the slums of Harlem, from the calm of the East China Sea to the gales of the Sea of Japan…to the hurricane now brewing on the Potomac.

And when he's coming home next time, you'd best stay out of his way!

Yet do I marvel at this curious thing:
To make a poet black, and bid him sing!

About the Author

Washington, D.C. native Christopher Chambers is a Professor of Media Studies at Georgetown University. His concentrations include mass media and technology's affects on politics, race, culture, science and environmental issues reflected in digital media, and media law. He is an on air analyst and commentator for TV and radio.

Professor Chambers is the author of the best-selling Angela Bivens series for Random House, co-editor of *The Darker Mask: Heroes from the Shadows* with Gary Phillips, and contributor to the collection Black Pulp. He is also historical advisor to the upcoming 1920s graphic novel, *The Ren*. He was a PEN/Malamud finalist for short fiction.

THE ALL-NEW *WILD* ADVENTURES OF

DOC SAVAGE

Doc Savage:
The Desert Demons

Doc Savage:
Horror in Gold

Doc Savage:
The Infernal Buddha

Doc Savage:
The Forgotten Realm

Doc Savage:
Death's Dark Domain

Doc Savage:
Skull Island

Printed in Dunstable, United Kingdom

68463289R00107